CRAZY ON YOU

BETTY PAPER

CRAZY ON YOU

CAPTIVE

1

Sergeant Major Sofia Pia Martinez examined the newly captured prisoner hanging naked and blind-folded in the middle of the room, his hands tied above his head to the main beam of the small building. He was a large man. She circled him again. A *very* large man, his flaccid cock reaching mid-thigh. Muscles bunched as he tried to turn himself to follow her movements. The tattoos that ran across his shoulders, back, and chest told of his time in the military. Her soldiers had done well in seizing such elusive, hard to catch prey.

He was believed to be a CIA operative sent to the small coastal country of San Pablo in South America to spy on the movements of the San Pablo Army near the country's main harbor. No ID was found on him so she didn't know his name. He hadn't spoken at all during his capture and subsequent binding. *How much does he know? How many operatives did the US send and where are they hidden?*

It would be her job to get those answers from him by any means necessary.

On her next pass she put her hand on him, running her

fingers along the chiseled flesh. His muscles rippled under the wake of her touch. He liked it. By the slow rising of his dick he liked it a lot. She brushed across his cock, making it twitch. His Adam's apple bobbed and his breath grew short. But still he said nothing, asked for nothing. She explored his body with both hands now, indulging her curiosity. The firmness of his ass, the power of his thighs, the indents of his hips that arrowed straight to his groin, the strength of his arms, and the softness of his lips. Heat rose within her and she ached to relieve herself with this fine male specimen.

His cock rose to full staff, jutting out proudly from his body. He didn't seem embarrassed or particularly surprised by his reaction to what she did to him. He owned it. Thrusting his hips forward, he all but commanded her to jerk him off. So she did. Slowly at first and then catching his rhythm, she stroked him faster with both hands. His chest rose and fell with each rapid breath. He was a marvelous creature. Beautiful. He would make a great pet as she extracted the information she needed from him.

He was close to coming, the pre-come weeping down his shaft, lubricating her pistoning hands. His nostrils flared as he grew closer and closer to orgasm. So close now. She could see it in the taut lines of his body and the firmness of his jaw. He pressed into her hands, chasing the pleasure she gave him. His lips parted.

She let go, leaving him on the edge of release. He gasped, his breathing harsh in the quiet room. She stood back and observed as he dealt with what she'd done to him. He was angry and if possible, *more* turned on. He liked having her in charge. He liked that she'd left him in this torturous state. This boded well for the time they'd spend together. As did his stamina. She slid a hand into her pants, sliding it across her clit, stroking herself, gauging his reaction as her scent filled the small space.

He took a deep breath in and she knew the moment he smelled her. His jaw clenched. Fondling her breast through her shirt, she tipped her head back and moaned. It was her turn to be right on the edge, her pussy dripping. She thumbed her clit, rubbing it hard and fast. She came on a broken cry that ripped an answering groan from him.

She circled him again, trailing her wet, sticky fingers over his body. On the last round she stopped and slipped her fingers into his mouth so he could savor her, want her. He sucked them in deep, making a noise as though he liked the taste of her. Her pussy throbbed in time with his suction. She wanted his mouth on her, wanted him to drive deep into her, forcing her legs wider as he pounded harder and harder.

All in due time.

First she had some information to gather on him so she could be fully informed before formally beginning his interrogation. She slid her fingers out of his mouth and slapped his ass. He twisted his body, following her movements as she left him alone with a dick hard enough to cut diamonds and the taste of her on his tongue.

2

CIA Special Agent Jake Callaghan knew three things about the woman sent in to make first contact with him—she held a high rank in the San Pablo army, she knew her way around a man's body, and she tasted like heaven. The second two worried him much more than the first. He wanted her to come back as much as he wanted her to never return. There was more than one way to break a man and this woman likely knew them all. And she was bold. He liked that. He also liked the way she took charge from the moment she entered the room, letting him know she was his dominant in *every* way.

He suppressed a shudder at the things she'd done to him, his cock still as hard as the moment she stopped stroking him. His balls ached so bad he wished she'd beaten him instead. Of all the people they could've sent in, they sent *her*. The scent of her still lingered in the air. He wished he could've seen her face when she came. He wished he could've seen her, period. All he had to go on was the feel of her hands and the taste of her pussy.

He didn't know how long he hung there after she left,

but he imagined it had to be nearly dark now, almost twelve hours since his imprisonment. Parks would've reported back about Jake's capture. He could only imagine how Parks would spin it to make himself look good and Jake look bad. Jake had been seized saving Parks's sorry ass. Jake wouldn't have gotten so stupidly close to the Army's base camp, but this was Parks's first mission and he had something to prove. All Parks proved was that he was a bumbling ass and Jake shouldn't have wasted his time saving the idiot. Then Parks would be the one hanging by his hands and suffering from blue balls.

The thought of Parks being touched by the woman made Jake instantly and insanely jealous. Stupid. It was so fucking stupid. He didn't even know this woman. He wouldn't even be able to pick her out of a line up, but the thought of her with someone else, making someone else submit to her was more than Jake could bear.

The door opened. He turned toward the sound. Since they'd blindfolded him, his other senses had kicked in to cover the deficit. Which had made what the woman had done to him all the more erotic.

The woman was back, but she wasn't alone. She circled him as she'd done the first time she'd been here. His body tuned itself to her and her every movement. She stayed just out of reach as though he'd free his hands at any moment and grab her. Or maybe it was she who needed the distance, the extra space to control her impulses. She gave a command in Spanish to the other person in the room. The other person—a young man from the sound of it—said something about Jake's hard-on. The woman told him to save it for last.

Jake schooled his reaction. He wasn't attracted to men, but the thought of another man touching him while she watched did strange things to him. If it was possible, his dick got even harder as the young man began washing him, starting at his feet in slow, methodic motions. He skirted around Jake's groin area and Jake imagined the young man on his knees in front of him, his face close enough to take Jake's dick in his mouth.

Jake tilted his head back and breathed deeply as the young man ran the cloth over his stomach and chest. The young man's body came up against Jake's as he reached up to wash Jake's arms. The two men were groin to groin. Bathing Jake turned the young man on. He could feel the other man's hard-on as it rubbed against his own. Jake turned his head toward where he knew the woman stood and ran his tongue across the seam of his lips. Her taste still lingered there.

The young man lowered his arms, letting his hands glide down Jake's body. The woman ordered the young man to wash Jake's hair next. She wanted him clean. He was being primed, but for what? When the last of the soap had been rinsed from his hair, the woman ordered the young man to his knees to finish washing Jake. The young man started from the front, drawing the cloth up Jake's left thigh and around to his ass. Jake's hardened cock rubbed up against the man's face over and over as he made his movements. Controlling his emotions, Jake waited for the young man to wash his groin area next. All the while, Jake followed the woman's movements around the room as though he could see her.

The sound of water sloshing in the bucket as the young man rinsed the cloth at Jake's feet was the only sound in the room. He held his breath in anticipation. The cloth was cold on his hip, the water having long since grown tepid. Jake shivered and he could almost feel the woman grin at his reaction. The young man ran the cloth between Jake's legs, massaging his balls. The hot breath of the young man on his dick was more acute in contrast to the cool cloth. Jake imagined the woman's wet pussy pulsing in time with the throbbing of his cock. She'd fuck like a champ. He'd bet on it.

The woman gave the command in Spanish for the young man to stroke Jake's dick. Faster, she said. Jake focused on anything except what the young man was doing to him. The woman continued to circle the room until she was behind him and he couldn't turn his head her direction. She told the young man to take Jake's cock into his mouth. The young man sucked him deep, eliciting a reluctant groan from Jake. Kicking Jake's legs apart with her own, the woman pressed against him from behind. She circled his anus with a wet finger, preparing him for her entry.

He was close to coming, but there was no way he'd allow himself to. She slipped a finger into his ass, angling it so it hit his P spot. She told the young man to stroke Jake's balls and take him deeper into his mouth, timing her strokes to match.

"Come," she ordered Jake in English.

Jake groaned, coming so hard his whole body jerked. All he could feel was the rush of semen leaving his body and the roar he made as she thrummed his P spot. Sagging in the aftermath, the ropes binding his wrists bit into his flesh. His cock slipped out of the young man's hot mouth at the same time the woman removed her finger. She praised the young man in Spanish, promising he'd be rewarded later. The door opened and closed and he knew he was once again alone with the woman.

She touched him, running her hands freely over him as though she owned him. And maybe in that moment she did. He'd never come so hard in his life. She traced the tattoo over his heart of an eagle. He could smell her arousal. If he could get hard again in that moment he'd be stone. She licked the wings, fanning out over his pierced nipple, and bit down on it. He jerked on the ropes.

The door opened and the aroma of food wafted toward him. He hadn't had anything to eat in over twenty-four hours. The door closed again and he knew it was just him and the woman. She pressed a spoon to his lips. He opened his mouth. Something spicy and beefy made his mouth water. He chewed and swallowed, then opened his mouth for more. The woman complied until he could hear the spoon scraping the dish clean. She wiped his mouth with a cloth. The dish clinked down onto a hard surface.

All of his training hadn't prepared him for this kind of treatment. There was more than one kind of torture. Wanting this woman and hating her at the same time was almost more than he could endure. She moved around the room again. He tracked her, following her movements. She stopped somewhere near the vicinity of the door and rapped on it. It opened. Someone else came into the room and approached him. He felt something cold, hard and metallic on the underside of his dick, making him flinch.

"*Hace pis?*" a young man different from the one before asked.

Jake turned toward the woman, pretending he didn't understand the question. The less his captors knew about him the better.

"Do you need to urinate?" she asked.

In response he peed.

"*Hace caca?*"

"Do you need to eliminate?" she translated.

Jake shook his head.

The woman ordered the young man to take the dish and

leave them. When the door closed the woman began her circling again. This time he didn't follow her movements.

She stopped in front of him. "What is your name?" she whispered in accented English.

Again he shook his head.

She cupped his balls, squeezing them. "What is your name?"

God, when she did that shit to him, he wanted to drop to his knees before her. Damn it if he wasn't getting turned on all over again.

"Jake." His voice sounded rough and gravely to his own ears.

"What are you doing in my country, Jake?"

"Vacation."

She laughed. "Mmm, and how do you like your vacation so far?"

"Beats visiting my family."

"And where is this family?"

"What's *your* name?"

"Call me Pia."

"Pia," he repeated, liking the sound of her name on his tongue. "Can I see you, Pia?"

She whacked his ass hard in response. He winced. She hadn't used her hand.

"What was that?" He couldn't keep the tremor of excitement out of his voice.

"Paddle. I ask the questions. What's your last name, Jake?"

"Callaghan." It wouldn't matter that he told her the truth. His name didn't appear on any documents in any country.

"Jake Callaghan. CIA? Military covert ops?"

"California."

WHACK!

He jolted, tugging at the ropes on his wrists. This hit harder than the last. His cock stiffened, his body reacting even as he willed it not to. She'd discovered his weakness. If a man had been in charge, Jake would probably be bleeding and spitting out teeth by now, and he'd keep his mouth clamped shut. But they'd sent in a woman. She'd pegged him right from the start. This sexual torture was far worse than any beating he could take. He wasn't sure how much he could endure without spilling everything about his mission.

"Do you want to fuck me, Jake from California?" she whispered near his ear.

"Yes." *Hell yes.*

"Earn it."

He registered the sharp point of a needle in his neck seconds before he blacked out.

3

Pia watched as her men secured Jake to the bed, splaying his naked body out. They cuffed his hands and feet to chains bolted to the floor at the four corners of the bed. He had a band around his waist that went through the bed and secured him to the floor. She lamented the need to put a tranquilizer collar on him. He had such a nice neck. One false move and he'd be out in seconds. She didn't trust him for a minute. They had found nothing on his DNA, fingerprints or his supposed name in any U.S. military or government agency's database. That meant he was probably black ops and even more dangerous than they originally thought.

Which made him valuable to his government and valuable to *her* government. He was quite the prize in more ways than one. She ran her gaze over his body, noting the marks and scars she'd been unable to see in the dim detention room. He'd been stabbed in the upper thigh. She fingered the six inch scar, still red, so not very old. The dark hair of his leg was just starting to grow back in around it. *What had he been through? Where did he come from?* He intrigued her.

When her men finished securing Jake, she gave the order for them to leave. All except Tito and Roman. Tito had earned his reward and Roman was the perfect prize. She should know. He was her most regular and faithful lover. He fucked long and hard and when she was in the mood, rough.

She ordered the men to strip. Tito hesitated. Out of shyness not reluctance, she noted. His eyes widened when Roman dropped his pants. His cock wasn't long, but it was thick and heavy and perfect for when she wanted it from behind. Roman eyed Tito's body, which was more on the slender, boyish side than she preferred, but she knew Roman would like his much smaller frame.

She sat in a chair next to the bed. "This is your prize, Tito," she said in Spanish. She always spoke to her men in Spanish. "And yours, Roman."

Roman moved first, grabbing the back of Tito's head and kissing him. Tito melted into him. Their bodies fit perfectly together. She'd seen the looks Tito had been giving Roman. She knew he wanted him. Roman was a man of few words, which he made up for in action. He was highly skilled both as a soldier and a lover. Tito's first time would be good, far better than most. If they wanted to continue their liaison after tonight, she would allow it. Roman glanced over Tito's head at her and his look told him more than the hard jut of his cock. He was grateful and his gratitude would mean glorious things for her the next time they were together.

Tito's hesitant touch seemed to inflame Roman. His hands were everywhere, caressing the young man's body as though he couldn't get enough. Tito gasped as Roman dropped before him and took Tito's dick into his mouth. The young man's knees started to buckle, but Roman clamped an arm around his legs holding him in place. Tito balanced himself on Roman's broad shoulders, his head thrown back in ecstasy.

Pia smiled. She liked seeing her men enjoy themselves. They worked long, hard hours, sometimes on no sleep. They deserved moments like this. So much of what they did was total and complete shit.

Jake made a noise and moved his head on the pillow. She'd taken the blindfold off. She wanted him to see her, wanted him to know who she was before she took things to the next step. And she wanted him to watch Tito and Roman. His head turned toward her as though his senses were automatically attuned to her and his eyes snapped open. He took in her appearance. To his credit he didn't flinch. The first time people saw her scar they were usually too shocked to school their reaction before she caught it. Not Jake.

His gaze traveled over her leisurely, no doubt cataloging her appearance for his superiors, should he have to recount it later. She'd taken off her shirt, leaving only her khaki green tank top on, showing off more marks on her body. Her breasts weren't large and they weren't small. She still wore cargo pants and boots, but soon those would go along with the tank top. First she wanted Jake hard and wanting.

"Hello, Pia."

"Hello, Jake."

His gaze left her and traveled around the room, snagging on Roman and Tito against the mirrored wall. Roman was on his knees behind Tito who was on all fours. He pressed his cock against Tito's asshole and slid slowly in. Roman murmured words of encouragement and endearments to the young man who had a look of sheer bliss on his face.

"I'm going to go slowly, pet," Roman told Tito in Spanish. "At first. Hold onto the chair if you have to. Tight."

The sound of grunts and flesh slapping against flesh filled the air.

Jake returned his gaze to her, but didn't say anything. His cock stirred, slowly rising. That was the only sign he gave that there was anything unusual going on.

"How are you feeling?" she asked.

"A little thirsty."

"In a moment." She waved him off, returning her attention to the men across the room.

Roman gripped Tito's slim hips, driving into him. She knew how it felt to have Roman inside her like that. What she didn't know was how he looked when he fucked. Like a god. His muscles bunched and flexed. She made note to use this room the next time they fucked so she could watch his face in the mirror. His usually hard expression softened, his attention fully focused on his task. Her pussy ached, wet and pulsing. If Jake weren't tied to the bed next to her she would've pleasured herself with one of the vibrators on the nightstand.

But she was saving herself for Jake. He watched her watching her men. Fully erect now, his cock nearly reached his midsection. It was a particularly well-formed cock and she wanted it inside her, filling her. Too bad she had to tie him down like that. She'd love to know what his hands felt like on her body. She'd bet he was an inventive lover and no woman would ever grow bored being with him.

Roman reached around Tito and pumped his cock. Tito came, shooting his come onto the floor. Roman thrust into the young man three more times and groaned as he too let his load loose into Tito. Yes, he was magnificent. Always a favorite of hers, Roman now slid up a couple of notches on her list. The men separated. Roman kissed Tito and praised him, calling him 'pet'. She supposed Roman was one of her pets so she could hardly be jealous of the endearment.

The men dressed, kissing between donning their clothing an item at a time. They laced up their boots and stood, waiting for her orders.

Pia rose and went to them. "Well done." She kissed them each in turn, with a hand on their cheek.

"Get the prisoner some water," she told Tito. When he moved away to attend to his task, she leaned up on her toes and spoke in Roman's ear. "You may keep your pet for as long as you both like, *mi favorito*." She bit his earlobe. "You've done well."

"Thank you, *Doña*." Roman cast a look of hatred at the prisoner tied to the bed. "What of him?"

"He's my concern, not yours."

"But—"

"You're excused."

Roman nodded, saluted her, and left the room. She excused Tito as well. And then she was alone with Jake.

4

Jake tugged on the restraints, making the chains securing him rattle. He watched Pia, Sergeant Major Sofia Pia Martinez—otherwise known as *La Vibora*, The Viper—stalk the room. If she was the one in charge here, then San Pablo was up to more than just moving surplus military equipment. A hell of a lot more. Oh, he'd recognized her, all right. She was infamous for being the only captive to successfully escape from a Columbian military prison. She was a ruthless, high-ranking officer of the San Pablo military. And she was beautiful. Remarkably so. The scar that ran from one corner of her face to the other, feathering into her hairline, giving her an unnatural part in her long black hair, did nothing to diminish her beauty.

She moved like a cat on long legs. Her dark eyes missed nothing. She had to know he'd recognize her. Which was probably why he wasn't wearing a blindfold anymore. It didn't bode well for his existence that she let him see her face. Her whereabouts had been something of a mystery since her escape. This was precisely the kind of information he'd been sent to acquire. His superiors would jizz their pants if they knew she was here.

"So, Jake from California." Her sexy accent rolled over him, sending a ripple across his senses. "I'll ask you again, what are you doing in my country?"

"Vacation. I'm having a splendid time."

She made a noise that was somewhere between a grunt and a growl and slipped a finger into his nipple ring, giving it a tug. "I know you know who I am." She twisted the ring. "I know you understand Spanish." The next turn of his nipple ring shot a bolt through him straight to his dick, bringing his hips off the bed. "And I know you're not here on vacation. Say that again and I will rip this right off your chest."

He could smell her perfume and her arousal, watching her men fuck each other turned her on. Tormenting *him* turned her on. He imagined her rising over him and sinking down onto his cock and riding him. She grabbed his dick, sliding her thumb through his pre-come as she gave the ring another small twist. Jesus fuck. He was so close to coming with nothing more than her hands on him.

She leaned down close enough to kiss. "Who do you work for?"

"I work at the Brainiac Bar, fixing computers."

She smiled, but it wasn't a nice smile. "So you know computers. Do you know what this is?" She held up some kind of rubberlike ring.

"Are you asking me to marry you?"

She gave his nipple ring a little tug, then released it. "*Sabelotodo.*"

He took a relieved gulp of air. But his relief was short lived. She widened the ring and slid it down his dick to the base. A cock ring. Her brief touch wasn't enough. He wanted her hands and mouth on him. She was the enemy, but he wanted her more than anyone ever. She would probably kill him when she got all that she could from him. The trick would be to give her just enough to stay alive and important, but not enough to jeopardize the mission and the other guys out there who he hoped were working on a way to get him the hell out of here.

She pulled her tank top off over her head, then unhooked her bra, letting it slide down her arms. Her nipples were shades darker than her brown skin and hard. He flinched, rattling the chains binding his hands. He itched to touch her, to draw her dusky nipples into his mouth and bite down on them. If she released him now he wasn't sure he could resist her lure over the need to escape.

Straddling his hips, she bent and did to him what he'd just been fantasizing about doing to her. He'd gotten the nipple piercing to please an ex-girlfriend. He had no idea it would make his nipple so sensitive or how much having it sucked would drive him insane. He rocked against her. Was she wet? Did she want to fuck him as badly as he wanted to fuck her? She lowered her body until her nipples brushed his chest. He suppressed a groan and almost missed her soft sigh. Hell yes, she was turned on.

She eased up and looked down at him. "I bet you're a good fuck. Most men with big cocks rely only on their size to pleasure a woman. But you..." She tapped a finger to his lower lip. "You don't. Do you?"

"No. And if my hands were free I'd show you." His dick pulsed, trapped between her clothed thighs.

"It's a shame to tie down all that potential, but we both know that's not an option."

"I've got the tranquilizer collar on. You could drop me before I could try anything."

"But maybe not before you killed or injured me. I'm not looking for any new scars."

The mark across her face wasn't the only damage she'd endured. From the looks of it she'd been tortured—beaten, whipped, cut, and God knew what else. She hadn't caved under all that abuse. And then she'd escaped, battered and bloody. There was a bounty on her head. Several governmental agencies around the world would love to know she was still alive, let alone her whereabouts, including his own. The stories about her were legendary. From what he'd seen of her in the short time he'd been her captive, most of them were true. She was known for inspiring unquestioning allegiance from the soldiers under her. He'd seen that first hand.

"They don't take anything away from your beauty." And they didn't.

"So I've been told."

She climbed off him and sat to unlace her boots, then stood and took off her pants. The scars continued to zigzag down her body. There wasn't an unmarked inch on her. What hell had she been through? It was a miracle she'd survived.

She strode to the other side of the room and looked at herself in the wall-to-wall mirror, hands on her hips. "I like them," she said, tracing a finger over one scar and then another. "I remember how I got each one. This one—" She touched a shiny, raised slash on her thigh that was eerily similar to the one he carried. "—barely missed my femoral artery. He was a nasty *pendejo*. He was also the first one I killed when I broke free. I used the knife he used on me to gut him like a fish."

She turned. "How did you get your scar?"

"Nothing as glamorous as your story. Although the end is nearly the same."

"Do you know why I wanted you instead of leaving you to my men to question?"

"My big dick?"

Stalking back toward the bed, her smile was wicked and sly. The kind of smirk that let a man know a woman was interested. "Yours isn't the biggest I've seen. Or had. No." She smoothed a finger across his scar. "It was this."

"What about it?"

"And this." She slid her fingernail under his nipple ring and tapped it up and down. "Why only one and not two? Did you... How do you say: *estabas intimidado*?"

"Chicken out? No. I don't know why."

"You weren't sure if she was worth going through it twice."

"Something like that."

"Something like that," she repeated as she straddled him once again, nestling the V of her pussy against the base of his dick where she'd placed the cock ring. "I think, under different circumstances, I could be the woman to talk you into a second one. No?"

"Yes, I believe you could."

She stretched out on top of him like a cat, sliding her hands up his sides to his arms until they were chest to chest. "What else do you believe I could talk you into?"

"Just about anything right now."

Rocking against him, he could feel how wet she was. "I think, Jake from California, that I'd like your cock inside me."

"I'd like that too."

She rose up and took his dick in her hand, stroking him.

"I will say this was a prize I didn't want to miss. But you, why do *you* want to fuck *me*?"

"Your taste."

She cocked her head to the side, dark hair falling over one breast. "My...? Oh. This?" She slid her hand between her legs and offered it to him.

He flicked his tongue out and licked. "Mmm, yes."

"I think that you would like very much to... How do you say: *comerme*? No?

He laughed. "Eat you. Yes."

"Is that so? Maybe another time." She glanced down to where his dick jutted up through her parted thighs.

Between her hand and the cock ring squeezing him, it was a slow kind of torture. Her strokes kept him hard yet he'd never come under such a slow pace. She had to know that and probably did it on purpose.

"Put my dick inside you. Ride me. I want to see you come. I want to *feel* you come."

She rose and positioned him at her entrance. His gaze locked on the sight of her hovering mere inches from impaling herself on him. Lowering herself, she wet the head of his dick with her slickness. Her scent was stronger now, the taste of her arousal still on his tongue. He focused on her movements, barely breathing. How could she remain so unhurried? His hips flexed upward of their own accord and he got caught in her opening for a fraction of a second before she shifted and he slipped back out. He growled in frustration.

"Who do you work for?" she purred, smoothing her hand up and down his shaft.

His gaze flashed up to hers. "Fuck you."

"As you wish."

She sank down on him all at once, the movement so

swift he sucked in a breath, nearly choking on his own spit. The muscles of his ass bunched, trying to draw his dick more fully into her. She put her hands on either side of his hips and used her full weight to immobilize him. If he wielded any strength to move her he'd only dislodge himself from her and that was the last fucking thing in the world he wanted to do right now. She felt so damn good.

"Jake, Jake, Jake," she singsonged. "What good is a large cock to me? I've got a half dozen at my disposal every day. Give me what I want and I'll give you what you want."

She squeezed his dick with her inner muscles and his eyes nearly rolled back in his head. He closed his eyes, trying not to think about her rhythmic constricting. More slow torture.

"Who do you work for?" she asked again, slipping a finger through his nipple ring.

"Told you," he panted. "Computer geek."

"Wrong answer." She reached behind her and massaged the ridged space between his balls and anus. "You like the way I make you come, no?"

"Yes."

"Do you want to come now?"

His hips jerked up in response. Her touch was expert. She knew a man's body, where to touch and how much pressure to apply to keep him right at the edge. He flushed hot, beads of sweat breaking out all over his body. Clenching his jaw, he suppressed the plea that wanted to spring up fully formed at the back of his throat. If his hands were free, he'd clamp her to him and pump into her, not stopping until she screamed his name. She increased the pressure of her finger. His knees bent, his heels digging into the mattress. He was so...fucking...close.

5

Jake was a large, magnificent man, a truly beautiful male creature who rode the cusp between controlled and feral. What would it be like to unleash all that power and have it directed at her? Being impaled on him, his big, hard cock throbbing inside her was maddening. More than anything she wanted his weight on top of her, pinning her to the mattress while he fucked the shit out of her, pounding into her until she lost her mind and went hoarse from crying out.

He jerked on the chains binding him. The tendons in his neck stood out proud, strung tight with barely suppressed anger and arousal. It was difficult to separate the two emotions in him at the moment. It worried her that a part of her wanted to ease his torment. He was glorious when he came, roaring like a rutting wild beast. To be the object of his desire must be a heady thing. She didn't dare imagine them beyond this moment. Did he?

"Who do you work for?" she asked again, then softer. "Tell me."

He shook his head. His dark eyes glimmered up at her in defiance. She didn't tolerate that in anyone. If he were one of her men she'd correct his behavior and make sure he never crossed that line again. But not Jake. She *liked* his obstinacy. She admired it. In that way, he reminded her of herself. This man would not break no matter what she did to him.

So why not enjoy him, while she had him?

She rose slightly, then sank back down. His eyes widened a fraction. She did it again. And again. That stubbornness held, but now it was mixed with something else altogether—longing. He'd imagined them like this. He wanted this. Hell, he'd demanded it moments ago. And now she was giving it to him.

She eased up until he nearly slipped out of her. "I will fuck you, Jake from California. You will come when I tell you to, do you understand?"

He nodded, his gaze never leaving hers. This was no truce. She was in control. She wanted him to understand that even as she rode him faster and faster. He met her with sharp, hard thrusts. She arched back, going hard at him, milking every ounce of pleasure from him. He more than filled her. He invaded her. Grinding her clit against him, she rubbed her nipples, pulling on them as she imagined he would if she allowed it. Her orgasm ripped through her. Beneath her, he moaned.

She gripped his face in her hands. "Come," she ordered.

He pushed up into her. His body went taunt, his hips flexing upward. The guttural sound he made was somewhere between a roar and grunt. She collapsed on top of him and sucked on his nipple ring, making him thrash in the aftermath of his orgasm. Yes, he was a mighty, beautiful creature. For a moment she imagined them under different circumstances as lovers, fucking every chance they got. He would be both relentless and generous, a rare combination. But this was a war and she was not free to take him or anyone else as a lover for any length of time. She was here today, but she could be halfway across the world tomorrow.

Jake raised his head and placed a kiss in her hair. The gesture both surprised and touched her. There was a tender side to him she wished she had more time and room to explore. Smoothing a hand along his chiseled jaw, she threaded her fingers through his thick dark hair and met his gaze. His dropped to her lips. She wasn't supposed to do this. There were rules. But his lips looked so soft and inviting. Her resistance against him already had cracks that were quickly growing into fissures. She'd given in to him and her own curiosity about him once. That was a dangerous precedent to set.

She lowered toward him. Just a taste, she told herself. A brief moment. Their lips connected and the brevity she'd promised herself got swept away by the low moan he let out. This man knew what he was doing. His mouth was exquisite. His tongue a gentle weapon he used with precision. A man who kissed like this knew how to use his mouth to seduce a woman. And he was seducing her. She knew it and didn't stop it. Why he put in the effort, she could hardly fathom. It wasn't to break free. She didn't know how or why she felt this from him, she just did.

He wanted her. His wanting had nothing to do with who they were or their current circumstances. It had everything to do with the chemistry between them. A man and a woman. A story as old as time. And yet, it went beyond chemistry.

He nipped at her lower lip. "It doesn't have a name," he whispered against her open lips.

At first she wasn't even sure he'd spoken. His words, breathed into her mouth, were little more than a sigh. Her heart rate doubled. He'd answered her question, giving her something to possibly use against him. She knew about the U.S. shadow organizations. It would be a matter of time and some digging, but she imagined she could find out exactly who he was and what he was doing here.

"You shouldn't trust me, Jake from California," she responded with the same soft, barely spoken tone. "I could kill you at any moment."

His answer was a flex of his hips, pushing his cock into her. He was still gloriously, deliciously hard. She gasped and he did it again.

"I want to touch you, hold you down while I thrust into you." He gave her another demonstration. "You shouldn't trust me, Sergeant Major. I could kill you at any moment... but I'd much rather fuck you."

He kept up the intrusion, languidly, yet forcefully letting her know how much he'd rather fuck her than kill her. Clasping his face in her hands, she kissed him. He didn't kiss like anyone she'd ever been with. Hell, he didn't fuck like anyone she'd ever been with. She grew desperate for the feel of his hands on her. What if she just released one hand? Either a voice command or the press of a button on her wrist unit would activate the tranquilizer collar. If things turned she could drop him in an instant. Tempting. Very tempting. With each roll of his hips she grew closer to orgasm and closer to the decision to free him.

She pushed up on his chest, needing to see his face. The ability to deceive was a skill he'd honed to perfection. She should know. She was also very skilled at deception and reading people. That's how she'd escaped the supposedly inescapable. He wasn't lying about wanting her. And she wasn't lying about killing him. But like him, she'd rather fuck than kill. Without breaking eye contact, she entered the code on her wrist unit that released all his bindings.

6

The shock of what Pia had done made Jake's brain slow to react. One minute he was bound so tightly he could hardly move. The next he was completely free with Pia still impaled on his dick. She watched him with sly, wary eyes that had seen more than they should have.

God, he wanted her.

His paralysis only temporary, he moved swiftly, switching their places. Suddenly she was beneath him, his dick still buried deep inside her. She made a sound that was a cross between surprise and delight. He held himself above her, his weight balanced on his forearms, bracketing her beautiful face. He could kill her before she'd ever be able to make a move against him.

But he didn't want to kill her.

He wanted to fuck her.

Maintaining eye contact, he hooked one of her legs, raising it, and changed the angle. He reared back and thrust so hard and deep, the whole bed moved. She clutched at him, drawing her arms and other leg around him, holding on tight as he drove into her again.

"Harder," she gasped.

Digging deep for purchase, he came at her with everything he had, using all his size and strength to propel him. The rapid-fire slap of skin on skin filled the room. The scent of her pussy wrapped as tightly around him as the real thing clasped his dick. She threw her head back and screamed as she came. He dug his fingers into the flesh of her hips, practically climbing her to get further inside as he too reached climax.

He fell heavily on the bed next to her, completely spent. His heart beat so hard he thought it might push its way out of his chest. Jesus god. He'd never come like that in his life. Too drained to move, he could only lie there and hope she wouldn't kill him. He'd be too slow to stop her.

Her hand smoothed up his arm and into the hair at his nape. She threaded her fingers through it slowly, experimentally, spreading goose bumps down his spine. Her touch was a balm. They were enemies and yet there was something basic and familiar about her that reached out to him down to the blackest, bleakest part of his soul. She understood him and he her. They'd seen and experienced shit no one should ever have to witness. Her, more so than him. And yet he didn't feel sorry for her. He didn't hate her. He *recognized* her.

"You are a good fuck, Jake from California," she announced.

He turned his head and smiled at her. "So are you, Sergeant Major."

"I would like to fuck you again."

He palmed her breast, running a thumb across her badly scarred nipple. "Give me a few minutes and I'll oblige you."

"That one doesn't feel." She shifted his hand to her other breast. "This one does."

Her admission was so matter of fact he almost missed the meaning behind it and then cursed out loud when the words finally hit. The asshole who had tortured her stole the feeling in her right breast. He'd kill the man if he were ever in the same room with the bastard.

He leaned down and kissed her marred breast.

"You're wasting your time with that one," she said.

"No. I'm not."

Something flickered behind her near-black eyes. She opened her mouth to say something, then clamped a hand on the back of his head and brought him to her for a kiss. Goddamn, the woman could kiss. And fuck. He was already feeling the stirrings of wanting her again. His dick pulsed, a halfhearted attempt at rallying back. How long would he have with her? Would it be long enough to do all the things he wanted to do with her?

She pushed at him and he raised his head.

"I have to go," she said, already trying to separate herself from him.

He looked down to where they were still joined. He didn't want to leave her, he realized.

She followed his gaze. "I will be back for more of this."

He gave her a quick hard kiss, then slid out of her and rolled free. He stood and stretched, not missing the way her gaze latched onto him and the movements he made. She enjoyed more than the way his body made her feel, she liked the way it looked too. He knew most women liked his body, but she looked at him as though she owned it *and* him. And damned if she didn't.

"Keep looking at me like that and I might not let you go."

Her frown was quick and fierce. "I have to ask something of you." Her gaze shifted to the bed.

"You have to tie me down again."

She gave a curt nod.

He did some more stretching, exercising under-used muscles. Her gaze never left him, hungrily following his movements. He did his best to knock out some of the kinks, then lay in the bed and held still while she refastened his restraints. When the task was finished, she looked down at him with a mixture of regret and longing. He watched her dress. Her movements were efficient. She was military through and through. He wanted to ask when she'd be back, but held his tongue. He needed to remember they weren't lovers. They were enemies. He was her captive, her prisoner. And this was war.

She laced up her last boot and stood. "I'll send someone in to bathe and feed you."

He didn't answer. What was there to say?

She gave him one last lingering look, then left without another word. He closed his eyes and huffed out a breath. He didn't know how long he dozed. Time meant nothing here, with no windows or clocks. He wasn't even sure how many days he'd been in captivity. No more than four, maybe five if he had to guess.

The door opening woke him even though it made no sound. His senses finely tuned to any change in the room. He could go from dead asleep to wide-awake in a second. His life had depended on that skill more than once.

The larger of the two fucking men from earlier came into the room and closed the door behind him. The soldier didn't bring anything with him so he wasn't here to bathe or feed Jake. What did he want? The look on his face made Jake wish more than ever to be free. He strode straight to the bed and ran his gaze over Jake. Jealous. He was jealous of the attention Pia had shown Jake. And angry.

The man moved swiftly, capturing Jake's throat in his meaty hand. "You fucked her," he said in Spanish and then spit in Jake's face, digging his fingers in deeper. "I can smell her on you. Your dick is still wet from her. Fucking asshole."

"Fucking coward, choking a man who can't fight you back," Jake managed in English.

The man didn't seem to understand the words, but he clearly got their meaning because he let go. Jake coughed, turning his head to take in more air.

"Roman!" Pia stormed into the room. "What are you doing in here?" she asked in Spanish.

"I've come to check on the prisoner."

"Is that the task I assigned you?"

"No, *Doña*."

She crossed her arms over her chest. The stare she gave Roman made Jake tense on the man's behalf.

The soldier shot Jake a look that said he'd be back and approached Pia. "I wanted to make sure he was secure. For you."

"By putting your hand on his neck and threatening him?"

Roman's head jerked back in surprise. So the room was being videotaped. Pia had been watching Jake sleep or else she wouldn't have known Roman had entered the room.

"I was—"

"Liar!"

Roman bowed his head. The deference he showed Pia spoke volumes about her control over her men.

"You have lost your reward. You will report to the infirmary for the next week. Let's see if emptying bedpans gives you any empathy toward those who cannot help themselves.

At the end of the week you will report to my quarters for your final punishment."

Roman looked as though he might argue, then thought better of it. "Yes, *Doña*."

"You will have to earn back my trust and respect. And your place."

He glanced up at that. "But *Doña*—"

She put up a hand, silencing him. "You would be wise to leave my sight. Now."

He saluted her and skirted around her and out the door.

"Are you all right?" she asked Jake in English when the door was firmly shut behind her.

"My face has some spit on it, but otherwise I'm fine."

"My apologies." She used a corner of the bed sheet to wipe his face. "Roman forgets his place sometimes."

"He's in love with you."

"Yes and he has a bad temper. It's unfortunate."

"The love or the temper?"

She sighed. "Both. But mostly the love. There is no place for that here."

"You fuck him."

"From time to time."

"How many of your men do you fuck?"

"You're not jealous like Roman, are you?"

"I'm curious." *And* motherfucking jealous.

"How many men and women have you fucked?" she asked.

"I didn't ask you about fucking women."

"Women don't have cocks. They are worthless to me for fucking."

"You've never had your pussy fingered or eaten by a woman?"

A corner of her gorgeous mouth turned up. "I have, but it's still not a cock. Have you ever fucked a man?"

"No. Men don't have pussies. They are worthless to me for fucking."

Her laugh was quick and throaty. "You seemed to like the mouth of a man on your cock."

"I was imagining it was your mouth."

"Would you like my mouth on your cock right now, Jake from California?"

"Yes."

She climbed onto the bed between his spread legs. "You have not been bathed."

"No. And my dick is still wet from you."

"I don't—how do you say—*no chupo la polla*?"

"You don't suck cock? Not even mine? Why?"

"I have better uses for a hard cock."

Now it was his turn to laugh. "Indeed you do."

He was hard as stone and aching for her. She eyed his stiff dick as though it was a treat she'd been looking forward to. Grasping it in both hands, she used her own remaining juices to stroke him.

He groaned. "Suck me off."

She raised one eyebrow.

"Please," he begged.

"And then what would I do? No more hard cock. A waste."

"Fuck me then."

"No."

He flexed his hips, thrusting through her slick fingers. God, she felt good. Everything she did to him felt like the first time. She was funny, smart, strong, and sexy as hell. He could see why Roman had fallen in love with her. She stroked firm fingers across the base of his balls, while jerking him off with her other hand. He was going to come, his jizz running through her fingers and down his dick. His breath came in short pants.

"You are a beautiful man," she whispered. "Magnificent. You give your coming everything you have. I like to watch it. Come for me, Jake."

"But it would be a waste," he gritted out.

"You are right."

She stopped. Everything. He gasped at the abruptness of it, suspended on the edge of orgasm.

The bitch smiled. "I will finish that when I have time." She climbed off the bed and looked down at him. "I want you behind me when next you come. Would you like that?"

"Yes," he panted.

She bent and licked his dick from base to tip in one long, slow swipe. He jerked on his bindings. It wasn't enough. At the same time it was too much.

"Until then, Jake from California."

The friction of her damp pussy against the roughness of her pants only made the aching worse. Pia thought of Jake with every step she took. Her superiors weren't happy with the progress she was making with her captive. She hadn't told them everything she knew about Jake. But they believed her when she told them she would get them what they wanted. Jake's life depended on the balance she struck between feeding the generals enough intel to make them happy, while withholding enough information to insure Jake was worth keeping alive. For the moment.

Her window was quickly closing. They knew as much as she that the longer they let Jake live, the more time they gave his government to launch a strike to get him back. It came down to his life or the lives of her men. She would choose her men over anyone or anything, but the thought of losing Jake was a burden she didn't want to bear. There had been something hot yet tender about the way he'd kissed her scarred breast. She'd long ago resigned herself to the damage her body had sustained. She was a survivor and survivors focused on the wins, not the losses.

When she came into the room where Jake was being kept, she found him awake and alert, his attention fixed to the door. If he'd been sleeping before she'd opened it, he gave no sign of it. In a different time and a different place she would've liked to keep him, explore him. For him she'd consider monogamy. If she had him whenever and wherever she liked, she'd never need another man.

"Hello, Jake."

"Hello, Pia."

"You are clean and fed?"

"Yes."

She strode to the bed and ran her gaze over his body. His cock stirred, growing to an impressive size. She worked the buttons of her shirt and pulled it off to reveal her bare breasts. His eyes were hot and hungry, following her movements. She made quick work of getting rid of her remaining clothing. Her pussy dripped from his look alone and her own expectations. This man rutted like a stallion and soon he'd be fucking her.

She lay in the bed next to him and ran a hand over his body, across his chest and lower.

"Have you come to fuck me, Pia?"

"I have."

"That wasn't fair of you to leave me like that."

"Will you have your revenge?"

"I will."

She released his bindings. He gave her a startled glance, then quickly got to his feet on the other side of the bed. She watched as he worked muscles he hadn't used in days, stretching and flexing. She regretting having to keep him bound. It was like keeping a proud lion in a cage where he paced back and forth, all that suppressed power and energy confined and unused.

He grabbed a couple of pillows, put them in the middle of the bed next to her, and pointed. "On your stomach."

She arched a brow, then slowly complied. With her ass stuck up in the air, she craned her neck to watch what he would do next. He climbed onto the bed behind her and smacked her ass. Hard. She started and was about to scold him when he put his open mouth on the sting and sucked. An electric jolt shot through her straight to her pussy.

"That's for leaving me hanging earlier."

She liked his idea of revenge.

He lay over her, covering her with his much bigger body, and whispered in her ear. "I'm going to fuck you so hard you won't be able to come again with any other man without screaming *my* name." Sliding a big hand between her legs, he groaned. "Fuck, you're wet."

He slipped a finger into her pussy, pulled back then added another and another until he fucked her with all four. She gripped the sheets, pushing back against the onslaught. He ripped an orgasm from her and chuckled when she pushed her face into the bed to cut off screaming the rest of his name.

Smoothing his hands up the back of her thighs, while she fought to regain her breath, he murmured wicked, vile things to her. She'd set him free and now she was the one imprisoned, unable to do anything more than lie there and let him have his way. His hands roamed freely over her, up her back, across her arms and down again. All the while his mouth moved, talking and licking and sucking. She trembled beneath him. There wasn't a place on the backside of her body he hadn't touched. His cock bumped against her, reminding her that he'd brought her all this pleasure without taking any for himself.

"Fuck me," she begged.

He gripped her hips. "How?"

"Hard. Now."

He kept a hand on her as he wet the head of his cock with her moisture. He pushed into her slowly, rocking his hips, his fingers digging into her flesh. She pushed back against him. He slid out, then in, agonizingly slow. The pressure gradually built inside her. She'd been looking forward to this for the past two hours. He wasn't going to cheat her.

"Harder, you bastard."

He laughed. "As you wish."

And then he let loose on her, fucking her so hard and fast she couldn't catch up. All she could do was hold on. She screamed. He just kept coming at her, pounding relentlessly into her. She came a second and a third time, but he held off. Sweat dripped off him onto her. Their grunts and the slap of flesh filled the room. He fucked like his life depended on it, like a goddamned champion. Reaching between her legs from the front, he strummed her clit.

She cried out. Her whole body shuddered in climax, this one stronger than any of the others. He thrust deep, roaring as he too came. He dropped next to her, his big sweat-slickened body sliding off to the side of hers. He had her pinned. His cock throbbed within her. She couldn't move, couldn't speak. Her breath came in short, choppy pants. She'd never been fucked like that. She had no idea it could be like that.

"When I'm sure I'm not going to die from a heart attack I'm going to turn you onto your back and finish what I started."

"You're not done?"

"Not by a long shot, Sergeant Major. I want my mouth

on you. Here." He moved his thumb on her clit. "And here." His finger dipped into her pussy. "And here." He worked his other hand under her, over her good breast. "And then I'm going to drive my dick into you and fuck you again."

His words sent a thrill through her she didn't think she'd been capable of after such a thorough and complete fucking. She pushed a lock of hair off his face. There was something about the way he looked at her in that unguarded moment. If they'd met under different circumstances she'd take him as her permanent lover. Or at least until she grew tired of him as she always seemed to do. Although she had a feeling she'd never tire of looking at him, let alone the magic he coaxed from her body.

He shifted, putting his forehead to hers. "How long will you keep me?"

Had he read her thoughts? No. He was asking a different question entirely.

"How many of you are out there?" she responded. It was best to keep some perspective here. She had a job to do.

"I'm vacationing alone."

That was bullshit. "How much do you know about what we're doing here?"

"Enough to get you off multiple times."

"Not an acceptable answer. Don't, how do you say, *no jodas conmigo?*

He smoothed his big palm over her ass. "But I like fucking with you."

"We're leaving soon. You won't come with us," she whispered.

His expression didn't change, but she knew he understood her meaning.

"Then I'd better get to work on your other side." He slid

his cock out of her and came up to his knees on the bed. "Roll over."

She complied, her ass on the pillows, raising her hips.

"I think I almost like this sight better than the last." He rubbed his thumb across her slit, mixing his come and hers together.

Her legs shook from all the orgasms he'd made her have. He pushed her legs further apart, staring down at her pussy.

"I've been waiting to do this since I first tasted you on your fingers," he said.

He licked her with the flat of his tongue from bottom to her clit. Gasping, her hips flexed off the pillows. He shoved his hands under her thighs and clamped down on her so she couldn't move her pelvis. His mouth tortured her fully sated pussy. Before she knew it, he had her barreling toward orgasm again. She jerked against his hands, wanting it to stop and to go on forever. It was a full out assault. This man was more skilled than any other man she'd ever met. She screamed, her voice raspy from exhaustion.

He gave her front side the same attention he'd given her back. His hands and mouth were everywhere. She thrashed beneath him, but he didn't let her come. Again and again he brought her to the brink. She begged him to let her go over, but he just laughed and then would do something to her that locked the pleas in her throat.

"Please," she begged.

He lowered his face to hers and kissed her gently, almost lovingly, taking his time. She wound her arms around his neck and held him to her.

"You're so beautiful," he whispered. "So strong."

"Come into me, Jake. Now."

He worked the pillows out from under her hips and eased her down onto the mattress. His body covered hers totally, completely. There wasn't a part of her that hadn't been touched by him. He slid into her slowly. She felt every inch of him. He *made* her feel him as though imprinting himself on her so that she would never forget him.

She wouldn't. Not ever.

J ake pushed into Pia as far as he could go. Even then it wasn't far enough. There were parts of her he'd never reach, no matter how many times and how many ways he tried. He didn't want her to ever forget their time together. His own time was growing short. It wasn't her fault. It wasn't anyone's fault. It was just a part of his profession, a part of war, and everything he'd signed up for when he agreed to an op. She did a good job of covering, but he could see her regret. He had a few of his own.

Her black eyes were wide, watching, taking in everything about him, every movement he made as though she were committing them to memory. He didn't fuck her. He made love to her. Where their previous couplings had been about power and hunger, this one was about what they'd found in each other and what they'd take away when they parted. She caressed him softly, almost reverently, saying more with her body than she ever could with her words. Stroking into her leisurely with absolute intent and wonder, he too tried to impart what he could never say.

He eased her into orgasm slowly. She gripped him to her

as he buried his face in the side of her neck and came with her. Afterward they lay in silence. He'd have given anything right then to know what she was thinking. They didn't move for a long time. He nuzzled her neck and got a weak response in return.

"Did I wear you out?" he asked.

"Yes."

"In a good way?"

"In a *very* good way."

Her response pleased him so much he summoned the strength to raise his head and kiss her. She looked like a well satisfied woman, pink cheeked, her eyes heavy lidded and sleepy.

"You are a good lover, Jake from California."

"So are you, Sergeant Major."

"I will miss you."

"And I you."

"I'm sorry."

"I know." He lifted a strand of hair from her face and smoothed it behind her ear.

She traced the edge of his face with her fingertips. "I have to go."

He nodded and rolled off her. She caught his wrist. The look in her eyes said more than any words she could offer. He placed a hand on her cheek, smoothing his thumb across her hairline. This was goodbye. She wouldn't come to visit him again like this. The next time he saw her would be the last time he saw her.

Shaking off any feelings of regret, he rose from the bed and watched her do the same on the other side. She dressed with efficiency, her attention on her task.

When she finished, she faced him across the bed, taking up her mantle of authority once again. He could see her put it on the way she'd put on her clothing. He'd never known a stronger, sexier woman in all his life.

He lay down in the bed voluntarily and assumed the position so she could bind him once more.

She let out a long sigh as she leaned down to fasten his bindings. "Thank you."

He acknowledged her with a nod of his head.

She left without looking back. It was just as well. He might've said something to get her to stay, to have more time with her. It was better that things went back to the way they were supposed to be.

He thought about Parks and the rest of the guys on his team. Were they looking for him? Would they try to negotiate with the San Pablo government for his release? Would they storm the compound or walk away from the whole operation and him? He chased these thoughts around and around. There wasn't anything else to do *but* think.

Hours later, the door opened again. He didn't expect to see Pia so he shouldn't have been disappointed when she didn't appear in the doorway. The young man from earlier came in with a stack of clothes. Jake's clothes. Five other soldiers trailed in after him. They took up a position around him, guns drawn.

One of the men ordered him to dress in broken English as the other men tensed. Suddenly Jake's bindings were released. He rubbed his wrists as though he hadn't been free since being captured. He rose to his feet slowly, pretending to be stiff, and dressed slowly. His clothing had been cleaned and pressed. They'd been returned to him a hell of a lot nicer than when he'd put them on the day of his capture.

The man directed him to put his hands behind his back. Another soldier shackled his wrists and ankles while the others stood and watched, their expressions tense. Even bound the way he was, they never took their guns off of him. A short time later Pia came into the room. She'd changed her clothes and pulled back her hair close to her head. She spared him the barest of glances as she ordered one of the men to put a hood over Jake's head. The last sight he saw was Pia pursing her lips in a silent kiss for him.

Her goodbye.

Someone pushed Jake forward. The chains around his ankles clanked as he shuffled along beside the soldiers. He could sense Pia behind him, could almost smell her. He could guess where they were taking him. Would Pia take the shot or would she order one of her men to do it? Would she watch him die or turn away? Would he get to see her face one last time or would they leave the hood on, leaving him to die nameless and faceless?

He didn't know how long they walked or where, but it was a lot longer than he'd expected. Cement gave way to hard packed dirt, then the cushioned forest floor. They wouldn't even dig a grave for him out here. No need. The animals and elements would take care of his remains soon enough. He preferred that to rotting in a six-foot deep hole in the ground. At least the last thing he'd smell would be the jungle. The last thing he'd hear would be the animals and birds. The last thing he'd breathe would be the ripe, sultry air of the rainforest. If he were lucky, there would be a shaft of sunlight giving off warmth.

The party halted suddenly. Hands pulled him down to a kneeling position. He went without a struggle. He lifted his head to the sky. It was daylight and he could just make out the canopy of the trees from the open sky. He was grateful for the sunlight instead of the blackness that was night in the jungle. There was some shuffling around him and then

Pia leaned down next to his ear. He knew it was her by her scent.

"Goodbye Jake from California," she whispered. "I hope you enjoyed your vacation in San Pablo. Come back for another visit."

And then she was gone.

Keeping his head high, he tensed for what would come next. He had no regrets about the way he'd lived his life except that it hadn't been nearly long enough. There would be no funeral for his family, no grave for them to visit. They might not even know what had happened to him. He'd disappear as though he never was.

The jungle noises grew louder, the birds and other animals going back to their business. He listened hard for the sound of human presence.

Where was the shot? Why hadn't they killed him yet?

The air inside the cloth over his head grew unbearably hot. He worked to keep his breathing under control. What the fuck was going on?

The rainforest grew quiet again. He turned his head to find the source of the disruption. Footsteps. Coming from in front of him. Shouts.

The cloth was jerked off his head and he found himself looking up into Parks's face, his head haloed by the mid-day sun.

Jake blinked up at the man. "What the hell?"

Parks clapped him on the shoulder. "Welcome back, Callaghan."

Flannery joined Parks and the two of them helped Jake to his feet as Commander Santos approached.

"You were a tough chip to bargain for," Santos said. "I'm glad we were able to get you back."

"You negotiated for my release?" Jake couldn't believe it.

Behind him Flannery worked on Jake's bindings.

"Traded two of theirs for you, but I'd say we made the better bargain."

Jake rubbed his freed wrists. "I thought the San Pablo government didn't negotiate."

"There's always a first. Apparently you did a good job of pretending to be just a tourist in the wrong place at the wrong time."

Pia. It had to be.

When Jake's leg irons were removed they walked to the waiting vehicles and climbed in.

Santos rubbed his hands together. "I'm looking forward to what you have to tell us. We've been hearing chatter that Sergeant Major Sofia Martinez is in the area."

If Jake let on that Pia was in fact here, they'd likely bomb the entire compound to get to her. She'd saved his life. He'd repay the favor.

"I don't know anything about that," Jake replied. "They kept me bound and hooded the entire time."

As they drove away from the site that should've been his grave, Jake glanced back and gave a salute to the bravest, sexiest woman he'd ever meet.

TINSEL

CHAPTER 1

Christmas was my favorite holiday. If I could, I'd leave my tree up all year long, but my roommate wouldn't allow it. Little did she know I snuck Christmas in wherever I could. Like wearing Christmas nickers every day. Today's pair were candy cane striped and I wore a red and white lace bra to match. My lipstick was always red and my shoes always green. No matter what. I played holiday music in my car year-round and the perfume I wore smelled of pine and cinnamon. Holiday sweaters were an out of control addiction.

All my good memories were tied to Christmas so it was little wonder that I volunteered to play Mrs. Claus at the local mall as part of a special program for underprivileged children. My ample curves filled out the white fur-trimmed, red velvet dress that I had specially made for me. It was a struggle for the seamstress to corral my overly large breasts, but she somehow managed it. The last thing I wanted was for one of my tits to pop out in front of the kids.

The faux mall was decorated for Christmas from the parking lot light posts to the domed ceiling, and everything in between. Holiday music pumped from the speakers and everyone seemed to bustle about to begin their holiday shopping. The illusion was perfect. I whistled along with We Wish You a Merry Christmas, my spirits high as I made my way to the private party. Santa and I were to do a meet and greet for the organizers before the gingerbread house was turned into a photo booth to memorialize the foster children's visit with Santa. At least that was the set up.

A little person dressed as an elf opened the velvet ropes for me and bowed as I made my way into the cordoned off area for the event.

"Hello," I said. "I'm Marla. I'm here for the *special* event."

"Good evening, *Mrs. Claus*," he corrected, reminding that this was a fantasy. *My* fantasy. "Santa's expecting you." He led me to the entrance of the elaborately decorated candy house and gestured for me to go inside.

"Thank you...?"

"Adasser," he answered, his gaze roaming over my body like a caress. "At your *service*."

My nipples puckered at his blatant sexual innuendo and stare. Indeed, it was clear exactly how he'd like to *service* me. I licked my lips and returned his look, parting my legs ever so slightly. From where we were situated, the fake mall goers couldn't see us. Even if we could be seen, I didn't care. This elf was handsome. More than that, he looked as though he knew exactly how to please a woman.

"And just what kind of *service* do you provide?" I queried.

"Anything you like, Mistress. We've been instructed to see to your every need."

"My *every* need?"

His hands were hot on the back of my thighs as he ran them up my skirt. "Whatever you wish."

"What if I told you I want you to make me come? Right here. Right now."

"Then it would be my duty and pleasure to make you come." His fingers toyed with the lace edge of my panties. "As many times and in as many ways as you'd like."

"Lick me."

His eyes flashed with desire as he pulled my panties slowly down to my ankles. I stepped out of them.

He took them in his fist and inhaled my scent. "Mistress, you smell like Christmas."

I raised the front of my dress and widened my legs, exposing my bare pussy. He tossed aside my panties and stared. Beneath his costume I could see his cock rise to full staff. It was rather impressive the way it bulged toward me.

"Lick me," I instructed again.

Adasser ran a finger down, then up my slit. He was the perfect height. I wouldn't have to bend or sit for him to put his mouth on me. My breasts ached. As soon as I had that thought, a pair of hands reached around and clamped down on my tits, twisting my nipples through the plush velvet of my dress. Behind me another elf stood on a candy-covered crate. He licked my neck and I shivered.

"That's Goldir," Adasser said against my inner thigh. "His duty is the same as mine. To please you."

"Mmmm," was all I could manage as Adasser licked me from cunt to clit.

His clever fingers drove inside me. If it wasn't for Goldir holding me up, my knees would've buckled. Adasser's talented mouth clamped down on me. He sucked me like a candy cane, savoring me as though he couldn't get enough. Goldir lowered the zipper on my dress, freeing my breasts. I was ravaged in the most luxurious, scandalous way as the sounds of mall shoppers went on a foot away, and We Wish You a Merry Christmas changed to Silver Bells.

"I am Nestor," a third elf whispered in my ear. "I am also here to please you."

Goldir and Nestor ducked under my arms and latched onto each of my breasts, holding me upright. Their hot mouths were a gentle torture. Below, Adasser worked his crazy magic, adding a thick vibrator to the mix, thrusting it mercilessly into my hot, wet pussy over and over again. The sensations built and built. There was nothing to do but let them carry me away. I came, screaming for Saint Nick and bathing Adasser's face with my steaming cum.

I was a big girl. It took all three elves to support me, but they didn't seem to mind as they led me into the ginger-bread house. Inside they stripped me of my Mrs. Claus costume and underwear, then guided me up the steps of a huge four-poster bed plush with Christmas colored pillows. They arranged me like I was a queen on a throne. Their massive cocks tented their short green pants and I ached to see them.

"Undress," I ordered and the elves quickly complied.

The naked men surrounded me, bending to their knees before me.

"How may we be of service, Mistress?" Goldir asked, running his hand up and down his thick, hard cock.

"Elves make toys, right?" All three nodded at my question. "Show me your toys."

Nestor and Goldir leapt off the bed and retrieved a toy box, placing it on the bed at my feet. Adasser lifted the lid and peered inside. He motioned for the other two to join him and they spent a good amount of time whispering between them before selecting a device. No. *Devices*. They each held identical contraptions and crawled toward me, the tips of their dicks wet with pre-cum. I couldn't wait to suck them and taste their juices. But first I needed to come again and they knew it.

Adasser knelt on my left with Nestor on my right. They pulled my legs up, opening me to Goldir who knelt between my chunky thighs. Elvis's Blue Christmas, my favorite song, came through the speakers. I shivered in anticipation. *What were they going to do to me?*

They placed suction cups over my nipples and clitoris. Spreading my legs wider, the elves squeezed the pumps attached to the cups. The suction built, drawing on my sensitized skin and making it pulse. I'd never felt anything like it. All the while, the men murmured naughty, dirty things to me about how hot I was and how hard I made them. The evidence of their arousal dripped onto my shoulders and thighs. The cups grew tight and I gasped under the sensations. Goldir pushed his fat fingers, slick with lube, into my pussy, stroking my g-spot.

I writhed on the bed, my head lashing back and forth. It was too much. All of it. And yet, not enough to make me come. The elves knew it, their dark chuckles mixing with Elvis's crooning.

"What do you want, Mistress?" Nestor asked, his cock inches from my face. "We're here to please you."

"I want to come," I gasped.

Adasser shook his head. "The master said to only let you come once."

"What about what I want?" Oh god, I was so close it burned. The pleasure and pain was almost too much. "Make me come!"

"No. Not yet." A new voice.

I raised my head and looked down my body to where Santa stood at the foot of the bed. He wore his white fur-trimmed red suit, his bright blue eyes focused on my cunt as the elves pumped the cups one more time. I moaned with pleasure. Everything throbbed. Santa stroked his white beard with one hand, the thumb of his other hand hooked in his belt. He smiled. The look in his eyes told me he knew exactly how naughty I'd been and how naughty I could be. For him.

Goldir's finger slipped from my cunt and rimmed my ass. He pushed in slowly, allowing me to get used to his intrusion. My hips flexed off the bed. Goldir pushed me down onto the bed, holding me there. Two sets of hands caressed and soothed me. This was everything and yet it still wasn't enough.

I cursed. Santa's grin grew wider. He watched me with a predatory glare, all the while standing there as though he didn't care. The elves worked me over. Tears leaked out my eyes and still they didn't let me come.

"Santa, please," I begged.

He shook his head. The music changed again. We Three Kings. The elves stopped everything. My chest heaved with pent-up frustration. The suction cups were released. It was worse without them than with them. My pulse pounded in my clit and nipples. I wanted to touch myself but the elves held my hands.

The men moved to my head, lining up. They took turns jacking off on me, while Santa watched. First Adasser, then Goldir, then Nestor. Their hot, starchy cum bathing my face and mouth. I couldn't get enough and turned my head, gobbling up every drop. I sucked from their cocks until they deflated and they pulled away.

Santa slid his belt through the loops, folded it in half, and snapped it. "My turn, Mrs. Claus."

CHAPTER 2

The song All I Want for Christmas Is You came on as Santa handed his belt to Nestor and ordered him to tie my hands to the headboard with it. The other two elves held each of my feet, their chest hair tickling. I was more turned on than I'd ever been in my life. This was my ultimate Christmas fantasy—to be pleasured by Santa and his sexy elves.

Santa watched me with a predatory gleam in his eyes. Under his gaze I didn't feel fat and lumpy. I felt sexy and desirable. And if what was going on in his suit was anything to judge by, Santa's look was very real. He *liked* what he saw. As did the elves. All three of their cocks were already beginning to rise for round two. They got off on my nude body. I licked my lips in anticipation and tasted salty elf cum, which only made me hornier.

Santa's heavy boot steps echoed in the gingerbread house. My anticipation soared the closer he came. He propped his hands on his hips and ran his gaze down, then up my body. He pulled a scroll from the inside pocket of his coat and let it unroll. It hit the floor and continued on somewhere under the bed. I could clearly make out 'Naughty List' in reverse at the top of the page. He perused the list, feeding it through his hands until he stopped and pointed.

"There you are, Marla. Do you know what bad girls get for Christmas?"

My distended nipples hardened, puckering under his hungry stare. "C-c-coal?"

"Indeed." He tossed the list aside and held his hand out, palm up.

Nestor put something huge in his hand. Santa held it up to the light. It was a large, black glass two-headed dildo. The shafts were wickedly spiraled and *massive*. There was no way that thing was going to fit inside me. I shuddered at the thought of Santa penetrating me with it.

Santa climbed between my legs, his attention fixed on my pussy. Nestor dripped lube on both heads of the dildo. My whole body shook in anticipation. Santa ran a finger down my slit, humming in approval at how soaked I was. His wet finger slid from my cunt to my ass. He used gentle persuasion to push past my anal ring. My hips flexed at the delicious intrusion. His single finger became two, then three, then his whole hand. I jolted at each thrust, my arousal soaring.

He replaced his hand with the dildo, thrusting into both of my hot holes at once. I cried out in pleasure as he rocked it in and out of me, slowly at first and then quickening the pace. I moaned in bliss, so close to coming. Adasser and Goldir's scorching mouths clamped down on my nipples. Santa flicked my clit with his tongue and that was it. I lost it, screaming my head off as my whole body exploded in ecstasy. My arms jerked at my bindings. The leather of Santa's belt dug deliciously into my wrists. I'd have marks tomorrow. That thought brought on another banging orgasm as Santa and his elves continued to suck me.

Santa Baby played over the speakers as I came down from the incredible intensity of my coming. Someone untied my wrists and rubbed where the leather had bit into my skin, placing gentle kisses along the welts. Santa hovered over me, his chin wet from my juices. He seemed very pleased with my reactions and stroked himself through the velvet of his suit. I longed to see his cock and tried to reach for it, but he pushed my hand away. Rising to his knees between my bent legs, he unbuttoned his coat. Beneath it, his chest was magnificently chiseled. No bowl full of jelly whatsoever. I reared up and ran my hands over his sculpted flesh. He let me have my way with him. His skin burned beneath my inquisitive touch.

My fingers trailed down his abs to the fastening of his pants.

He stopped me. "Treats are for girls who've been good."

"I can be good, Santa." I pressed my hand to his straining erection, by far the largest in the room. It nearly rivaled the huge black dildo still embedded deep inside me. "I can be *real* good."

He reached down and slowly withdrew the dildo from me. I groaned. I was going to miss that lump of coal.

Santa put his arms out to his sides in invitation. "Show me."

I worked the button and zipper in record time. His long, thick, hard cock fell into my hands. The head was coated in pre-cum. Holding it in both hands, I swirled my tongue around the salty tip. He tasted better than any holiday treat, better than wassail on a cold winter night. I looked up to find him watching me, his focus on my lips rimming his cock. I took him deep. He put a hand on my head and pushed deeper into the back of my throat. I didn't think I could take that much of him, but somehow I did.

One of the elves positioned himself below me and another knelt behind me. The one in the back pushed his hard dick deep into my ass, while the one below me thrust into my pussy from below. I jolted and moaned around Santa's cock at the incredible double penetration. Santa jerked his hips, driving in and out of my mouth. Losing track of who was where, I dove head first into the immense pleasure as the third elf pressed a vibrator to my clit.

Santa shoved his dick into the back of my throat. I gobbled his cum as fast as he shot it. His deep groan rocketed me into orgasm. The elves pulled their dicks out and shot their wads all over me. I was bathed in hot, sticky spunk. Rolling to my side, I rubbed it into my skin, luxuriating in the feel of their arousal all over me. The four men stroked their shafts, emptying themselves onto me.

I'd never felt so wanton in all my life. Or so wanted. All four men collapsed around me, spent. It was going to take me some time to reignite my jets, too. I'd never come so many times in my life. I wasn't sure I could go another round with them, but as they stroked my body, their caresses both reverent and hungry, I knew I had to at least give it a try.

Besides, I wanted...no I *needed* Santa's big cock embedded deep in my cunt. Just the thought of it made my clit tingle in anticipation. Santa lay between my legs, his head on my stomach. I sifted my fingers through his soft white hair. I'd never seen that color on a man so seemingly young. Adasser and Goldir stroked my hair lazily while Nestor pillowed his head on my right breast.

I was eager for their cocks to re-inflate. We had hours yet and there were so very many sexual things I wanted to do that I'd never done. I couldn't wait to see what they had in store for me. Santa licked a trail down my stomach to my pussy and dipped his tongue inside.

"Like cookies and milk," he murmured. "If you were waiting just like this at my first stop I'd never get to the other houses." He winked up at me.

I widened my legs, inviting him. Nestor pulled my cunt lips apart, exposing my insatiable clit to Santa. The gentle suction he applied made me roll my head on the pillow and moan. Goldir and Addasser got into the game, licking my neck, sending shivers of arousal through me. I couldn't come again so soon. No way. But Santa worked his magic and in no time, I writhed on the bed, begging for release. It took all four of them to hold me down as Santa licked and sucked me into another screamer. Just as my orgasm peaked, he slapped my clit repeatedly, sending me deeper into my climax.

I collapsed, sure I was done for the night. "Please, no more," I begged.

"You'll take more," Santa assured me. "You'll take my cock up your beautiful cunt and you'll ride me as you sit on my lap and tell me what you *really* want for Christmas."

CHAPTER 3

I shivered at the promise in Santa's tone and the sight of him on his knees between my legs, stroking his enormous shaft. I worried I wouldn't be able to accommodate his size. I'd never seen a cock that big outside of a porno.

He must've seen my fear because he leaned down and kissed me. "It's going to be the ride of your life. I promise. Now turn over."

I didn't know what he had planned, but I did as he ordered. Goldir arranged me so that a pillow was under my pelvis, forcing my ass into the air. I had a moment of hesitation about my giant butt hanging out there, but those fears were assuaged when Santa called his elves over to his angle.

"Have you ever seen such a glorious ass?" he asked them.

"Never," Nestor answered, running a reverent hand over one of my giant white globes. "I could bury myself in this ass forever."

Goldir came to my other side and bit my cheek. I jumped at the sting, but he quickly soothed it with a lick and a kiss.

Adasser gave my ass a smack. "I'd fuck this ass all day, every day."

"Now that we've got her where we want her, what should we do with her?" Santa asked.

His question sent chills of desire through me. I rolled my nipples between my fingers and bit my lip. What *were* they going to do to me?

A hot tongue pressed against my anal rose. I gasped as Adasser rimmed my hole. Pleasure snaked through me and I pressed my face into the mattress, sticking my ass higher in the air. More. I wanted more.

Santa chuckled. "She likes it. Let's see if she likes this."

I felt the slippery intrusion of something circular slip past my anal ring. Then another. This one larger. Then a larger one still until I was full. I groaned. I loved ass play. The tongue returned, sweeping around the thick base of the anal beads. A hand reached between my legs and suddenly a vibrator was pressed to my clit and held there. Santa smacked my ass with the flat of his hand and held it over the sting. He slapped me again and again as the sensations built.

My cheeks burned. My clit burned. My asshole burned. I shouted when I came. The orgasm drew out longer than any I'd ever had before as the anal beads were pulled from me. I sagged on the bed, totally spent. I couldn't take anymore. There was no way. I couldn't even move.

"Turn her over," Santa ordered and the elves complied.

Four men with powerfully huge erections kneeled over me, looking down at me as though I should do something about their predicament. But I was too tired. As much as I wanted to, there was no way I could take care of them the way they'd taken care of me.

Santa leaned over me and kissed me. There was nothing

but sweet appreciation in his kiss. The elves kissed and licked my body, starting with my hands and feet and progressing up my limbs in turns—one man, then another. Santa kissed a path down my chest to my belly. My whole body vibrated under the onslaught. Despite my earlier doubts I could get aroused again, my chest heaved, my nipples puckered, and my pussy, my insatiable pussy dripped. They kissed and licked me everywhere except where I now wanted—no, *needed*—them to suck me. Writhing on the bed, I tried to relieve the pressure myself, but my hands were held, forcing me to endure the endless pleasure.

Santa lifted one of my legs, turning my body to the side. Pillows were shoved under me, lifting my lower body into the air. Santa positioned his dick against my pussy and teased, running his cock head back and forth in my dripping heat.

"What do you want for Christmas, little girl?" Santa asked.

"I want you to fuck me," I gasped. "I want you *all* to fuck me."

Here Comes Santa Claus came over the speakers as Santa pushed his huge cock into me, not stopping until he was fully seated. Trying to adjust to the intrusion, I gulped in air. The elves continued their oral assault. One of them sucked my toes while kneading my arch, which I found tantalizingly erotic.

Santa glared down at me as he slowly withdrew till his tip rimmed my pussy. He drove into me again in the same agonizingly slow movement. I knew it was for me. So I could adjust. But with my foot hooked over his shoulder and the elves finding sexual centers on my body I didn't know existed, all I wanted was to be pounded hard and fast.

Adasser exposed my clit and sucked on it. My head rolled back and I lost all sense of who was where doing what. Santa held me by my leg and picked up his pace, forcing his giant cock into me harder and harder. His body became slick with sweat. Too soon I cried out, my whole body going taut. Adasser's clever mouth drew out my orgasm to impossible lengths. I never thought it would stop.

Santa groaned and thrust deep into me, bathing my cunt in his delectably hot cum. I ached to taste it. He pulled out of me and I swung my leg off his shoulder and sat up so I could suck his cock. I gripped it in both hands and licked from the base to the tip, swirling my tongue across his salty head. He held my face all the while, telling me how beautiful and sexy I was. The elves joined in and I found myself swamped with male appreciation and desire like I'd never felt before.

When I'd gotten my fill of Santa's juices I flopped back on the bed. Again I was arranged on the bed, this time on my stomach. Parting my ass cheeks with sure hands, Nestor sucked the cum from my pussy, his thumb gently strumming my clit. Soon I was begging for him to fuck me. He thrust hard into me, gripping my hips. The other elves gathered around and encouraged him. His cock just kept coming, hitting my G-spot in a constant rhythmic motion.

I panted, so close to orgasm. He twisted his hips, the motion making him hit harder, and I came, crying out his name. He growled, shooting his load deep into my cunt. Two down. Two to go. I didn't think anything could get me going again, but the thought of more spunk running down the insides of my legs had me begging Goldir to be next. His cock was the shortest but the thickest by far. I yearned to be stretched by him.

Goldir stepped up behind me as soon as Adasser pulled

out of me with a smack on the ass. Without hesitation
Goldir thrust into me. I gasped and strained to accommodate him. He lunged at me over and over, his broad cock
almost unbearable. Santa straddled my back, careful not to
crush me, and fingered my anal rose. That's all it took for me
to begin barreling toward orgasm. Goldir stiffened and shot
his jizz into me. The pulse of his cock inside me did me in. I
came on a long, low moan.

As unceremoniously as he entered me, Goldir pulled his
cock out. Nestor was next. Santa leveraged off of me and
they rolled me onto my back. Santa laid my head in his lap
and wrapped my arms around his back, holding them in
place. Adasser and Goldir spread some kind of lubricant on
my cunt. As if I needed it with the hot cum of three men
dripping out of me.

But this wasn't lube. Oh, no. It was hot and tingly. The
two elves held me down when I tried to move. Nestor knelt
between my legs. He had a cock ring on with a vibrating
bullet positioned so that when he thrust into me, it would
pulse on my clit. Santa grabbed my tits in his hands. The
sneaky bastard had vibrating bullets that stimulated my
nipples. Nestor positioned himself over me and ran his cock
up and down my crack. His wasn't a sudden intrusion; it was
achingly slow and deliberate.

I couldn't help but stare at where our bodies connected.
Something flickered in his gaze, something I couldn't put
my finger on. He looked at me differently than the other
men had. Oh they desired me, but Nestor, he not only
wanted me, he cared about me. The realization made the
backs of my eyes sting. He wanted me to see him, to see how
he felt about me as he entered me.

He took his time, building me slowly toward orgasm. I
arched my back to take him deeper. I wanted this connec-

tion with him and I wanted him to know it. The other men and everything else in the room faded away in that moment. It was just me and Nestor. I gripped the headboard behind Santa, suddenly wishing he wasn't there, wishing none of them were there. This was my fantasy. I never thought in a million years that a man like Nestor could want me, *really* want me.

But he clearly did, whispering words of endearment, telling me how beautiful I was. A curl of his dark hair stuck to his forehead as he worked over me. I dug my heels into his back, encouraging him. Oh god, he felt good. *So good.* None of the others had felt like this. None of the others had looked at me the way he was looking at me. None of them made me feel this wanton or wanted. Who was this man? What was he doing to me?

The other two elves clamped their mouths on my nipples. The bite of the suction threw me over the edge and I cried out Nestor's name as I came. Nestor thrust into me several more times and then collapsed on top of me, his hot jizz pumping from his cock into my cunt. Our gazes locked and held over the top of the other men's heads. I wished in that moment that I knew his real name.

He pulled out of me, bent down, and placed a reverent kiss on the top of my pussy. I was spent. The men were spent. But we still had the rest of the night. I wondered how the tone would change, how what I'd just experienced would change the adventure. I couldn't send the rest of the men away and a part of me didn't want to. I'd paid for this sexcapade. I was going to see it through no matter what. Not even for a sexy elf with a dimple in his cheek and dreamy, chocolate brown eyes.

CHAPTER 4

They practically carried me to a tub that magically overflowed with hot, sudsy water that smelled like warm gingerbread and vanilla. The strains of Silent Night played gently in the background. They lowered me into the bath like a queen. Instantly Goldir appeared at my side with a tray of food. He slipped a delectable hors d'oeuvres between my lips that nearly made me sink fully into the water, it was so decadent and delicious. I didn't realize how much of an appetite I'd worked up with Santa and his elves until my stomach rumbled. Goldir chuckled and fed me another tasty morsel.

Santa sat on a stool behind me and kneaded my shoulders. At the other end of the tub, Nestor rubbed one of my feet while Adasser massaged the other. It was heaven. Between the raucous rounds of sex, the bath, the food, and my three handsome masseuses, I was in serious danger of drifting off. But this fantasy was only for one night. There was no way I was going to sleep through any of it.

Goldir gave me a beautiful fruity drink to sip that seemed to have some kind of stimulant in it because before I knew it I felt reenergized. Or maybe it was the food. Or the hands that had drifted from my shoulder and feet to the rest of my body. Their fingers were sin and soon I was flushed from more than the warm, scented water.

It had been so long since I'd felt desired and desirable that I'd almost forgotten what it felt like. But these men made sure I didn't doubt myself for even a second. There were some things that couldn't be faked like the four rock hard cocks pointed at me from every direction. I couldn't wait to see what they came up with next.

I was lifted out of the bath and stood still while the men toweled me off, paying extra attention to the parts of me they liked the best. Santa stood behind me, doing a bang up job of making sure my ass was good and dry. Goldir and Adasser stood on stools on either side of me, each making sure that my breasts were well and truly dry, which included a lot of sucking on my nipples, dabbing them dry, then repeating the process. Nestor rubbed the landing strip on my pussy until it gleamed and my cunt dripped.

I don't know what they had in store for me next, but whatever it was, I was ready.

They led me to a different room. This one had pillows all over the padded floor. Everything was white. Even the walls were padded white. All except one. They positioned me so that I faced the blank wall. Santa sat behind me and I reclined against him. The elves arranged themselves around me and didn't stop touching me. I parted my thighs and played with myself absently, swirling my fingers through my slickness. Nothing serious, but it felt good and I liked the way the men's cocks got suddenly harder, leaking their sticky cum on my freshly scrubbed skin.

Rudolph the Red Nosed Reindeer filtered in over the speakers as the blank wall turned clear, revealing scenery from the North Pole, complete with Santa's house and the elves' toy shop. A man dressed in a reindeer costume complete with a red nose was bent over Santa's sleigh. Another male reindeer, Comet, with a massive, and I mean MASSIVE cock stood behind him, slapping his bare ass with the reins of the sleigh. Every time the leather lashed Rudolph's skin, he cried out in ecstasy. Rudolph's own dick was granite hard and dripping.

Seven more reindeer came into view, each one sporting an impressive hard-on, but Comet's was by far the biggest. Dasher squirted Donner's dick with lube, rubbing it up and down so that his shaft was thoroughly coated. Comet stopped thrashing Rudolph so Donner could push his cock into Rudolph's ass. Next up was Blitzen, then Dancer, then Cupid. Vixen came next. Followed by Prancer, Dasher, and bringing up the rear (literally) was Comet. In unison they fucked each other. So these were reindeer games and this time Rudolph was getting to play.

Oh, boy.

The scene had a powerful effect over Santa and his elves. Their hands and mouths got very busy on my body. The music changed again to All I Want for Christmas Is You. I couldn't even focus on the reindeer scene because what was happening to me was way more interesting.

I suddenly found myself on all fours. Nestor climbed under me and buried his face in my pussy. His wicked tongue worked me over while Santa plowed my ass with his fingers, filling me in the most interesting way. I'd always enjoyed ass play, but Santa took it to a whole other level. I could feel my orgasm building from what he alone was doing. The other two elves attached clamps to my nipples with weights hanging from them. The tension stretched my nipples to impossible lengths, sending a wave of desire coursing through me.

Santa replaced his fingers with his cock and it was game on. I backed into him, momentarily dislodging poor Nestor who quickly rebounded, coming at me with renewed effort. He sucked my clit so hard, stars exploded behind my eyes and I came all over his face. Behind me, Santa pounded into me. The weights swung back and forth, intensifying their effect. I chased a second orgasm, caught it and somehow managed a third. Santa pulled his dick out and shot his spunk across my back.

A second cock pushed into me seconds later, this time in my pussy. Fucking Goldir, with his fat cock rubbing that sacred spot inside me, sent me to my elbows. I gripped the pillow for purchase. I wanted to feel every inch of him. Nestor rapidly flicked his tongue across my clit like a human vibrator. My inner muscles clamped down on Goldir's cock and I cried out, coming like a mother fucking freight train.

Goldir pulled out and pumped his hot cum on my ass, groaning so loud he drowned out the opening notes of White Christmas. And damned if I wasn't having a white Christmas of my own. All that jizz and none of it to taste. As soon as I had the thought, Nestor appeared before me and helped me back up to my hands. I latched onto his cock like I needed it to breath, sucking him down deep. Adasser spread the cum on my back and ass, into my crack, mixing the two specimens together. I moaned in approval.

Nestor held my head as he pumped his dick in and out of my hungry mouth. Using the natural lube the others had left behind, Adasser drove deep into my pussy, making an unmistakable squelching sound. Nestor's cock exploded in my mouth. I sucked him dry until he fell back onto the pillows, gasping for breath. The weights swung back and forth with Adasser's thrusts. Santa reached under me and tightened them, making me shout for God just as Adasser hosed me with his hot cum.

I fell heavily onto the pillows, mashing the nipple clamps tighter. The reindeer shot their wads in unison, splashing it all over each other. Holy hell. I'd never seen anything like it and likely never would. My insatiable cunt pulsed at the sight. The curtain closed on the scene. I'd never hear the song Rudolph the Red Nosed Reindeer the same ever again.

I looked around at my men. I'd worn them out. They lay about, glancing from one to the other, then to me. Around and around this went. What in the world was going on? Had something gone wrong? I couldn't fathom what it could be. I still tingled from their plowing and while their spunk had cooled, the feel of it coating my skin thrilled me.

I reached back and swirled my hand in it, then licked my hand clean. The men glanced from me to their cocks, which had taken notice of what I was doing and were rousing for another round. Each of my guys wore a look of utter disbelief and devotion. I rolled to my back and yanked the nipple clamps off. The scrape of the metal across my highly sensitized flesh made my hips flex. Never had I been so constantly and violently aroused.

Was it this house, these men or was it something that had been inside me all along? I'd enjoyed a fairly satisfying sex life—I had a stack of dead vibrator batteries to prove it—but I never dreamed in a million years that sex could be like this, that four insanely hot, virile men could be so into me or that I could fuck them into stunned devotion. The way they each looked at me left me a little breathless. A man had never looked at me the way the four of them gazed at me now.

One by one they moved toward me, backing me up against the padded wall of the room. They kissed me, one after the other. This adventure had taken a drastic and unforeseeable turn. I didn't know them, had never met them before walking into this fantasy, but I had a feeling our little sexcapade would leave each and every one of us changed. I didn't even know their real names. I held their faces as we kissed, letting each of them know how much our time together meant to me.

They lay down, surrounding me on all sides, caressing and kissing me. If I had to guesstimate, we still had a few hours left together. What would they come up with next?

CHAPTER 5

After a short rest, Santa picked me up and carried me into another room—Santa's workshop, complete with all manner of sex toys lining the shelves. Some I'd never ever seen before. I trembled in anticipation of what the men would do to me. In the center of the room a swing hung from the ceiling. Whoa. This was going to be good. My other three guys followed us in, then quickly disappeared. I had a moment of panic that they might not come back, which was fortunately short lived. They came back in, wearing these bizarre green cage things on their dicks and balls.

Santa lowered me into the swing and the elves went to work, helping him position me in it spread eagle. *Everything* was on display. They'd each had their hands and mouths on me and yet sitting alone in the swing in the middle of the room completely at their mercy was totally next level stuff I wasn't sure I was prepared for. Christmas Time Is Here played in the background as the elves busied themselves doing something I couldn't see. It involved hammers and saws and other tools I didn't know the name of.

Santa put the straw of a cranberry flavored drink to my lips. "Suck," he whispered suggestively as he straddled my torso, the white hair of his thighs tickling me in the most suggestive way.

He'd re-donned his red and white fur Santa cap while I wasn't looking. He had the same strange contraption on his cock in red that the elves wore. On closer inspection I noticed it had a vibrating bullet with little rubber nubby things on top that would hit my clit perfectly with every thrust. These guys were really taking it up a notch. The cage thing did amazing things for Santa's stiff dick, making it appear thicker and longer. I couldn't wait to find out how it would feel driving into me.

When I finished the drink he set it down and dove for my tits, palming them in his large hands. His thumbs rubbed my overly sensitive nipples and I jolted, making the swing rock. He smiled at me as he bent his head and flicked my tips with his tongue. That shot a pulse of pure pleasure straight between my legs. I moaned and pulled on the restraints, holding my arms above my head. I could easily free myself, but I'd much rather give in to the illusion of being tied up and at their mercy.

The elves returned, each carrying a chain that rattled. Santa blew on my wet nipples, making them pucker, before swinging his leg back over and climbing off me. Goldir attached a clamp to my left nipple while Adasser clamped one to my right. Nestor appeared between my legs and parted my folds. He sucked on my clit, drawing it out, and then attached a third clamp to my hood. Santa hooked all three clamps together, then put me in a gentle swing. The chains moved as I rocked, making the clamps randomly tug on my most sensitive areas.

Oh holy night, was it delicious.

The elves hustled over to their workbench and returned with the largest dildo I'd ever seen. It was red and made of some kind of jelly material because it bounced menacingly as they drew near me with it. They squirted it liberally with lube. One of them flicked a switch at the base of the balls and it started to vibrate. It took all three elves to hold it and position it at the entrance of my pussy.

Santa pushed me forward. I arched into it, dropping my head back as I was impaled. Full. I was *so* full. The thing vibrated so deep inside me I felt it all the way up to my throat. Santa pulled me back. The shaft raked my nerve endings, sending them jangling. The chains shifted and the clamps bit down at different intervals. Santa timed the swings, driving the dildo in and out of me in a steady, unrelenting rhythm.

I thought I was going to lose my mind. Of all the things they'd done to me, this was by far my favorite. My body jolted every time the dick was fully seated and I found myself craving its fullness like air each time it pulled out of me. I came almost instantly, screaming my head off. This was THE BEST orgasm I'd ever had. Probably the best I ever would have. I gasped in the aftermath, totally limp and spent.

Whatever they had in mind next would have to wait until I recovered my faculties. I think my brain shortcircuited. For sure, they'd done my pussy in. It would never be the same. Merry Christmas to me. I could die right now and float away on a cloud of bliss.

Christmas Time Is Here changed to Frosty the Snowman.

Oh shit! What was that? Something cold rubbed across my clit, then slid slowly inside. I leaned up to see what my men were up to. Adasser pulled an icicle that looked like it had been broken off an eave out of my pussy and licked it like a Popsicle. He handed it off to Goldir who slipped it into me and did the same. Nestor was next. Oh my naughty, naughty boys. The cold worked wonders to revive my poor abused vag. Watching my guys suck my juices off of it spiked my interest again. Such clever lads!

Santa set the swing into a gentle sway as the elves took their turns. The chains shifted, undulating in a random pattern. I never knew which one would tug next. Enjoying the sensations, I went with it, letting my guys have their fun and resting up for whatever they would do to me next. I'd never been so overly sensitized in my life. It was like someone had turned the volume on my world to maximum. Every movement they made, every touch, every sound and sensation was amplified. I would sleep for a week after this night and spend the rest of my life reliving it.

The swing picked up pace. Santa was no longer controlling it. With my pussy chilled, it took me a moment realize that they'd stopped using the icicle on me. Adasser's cock rammed into me. The cage thing he wore on his dick made it impossibly hard. With every stroke the vibrating bullet kissed my clit, tingling in unexpected ways. The intermittent tugs on the clips increased with the faster motion and I found myself barreling toward orgasm. It hit with the force of a runaway sleigh, slamming into me. I threw my head back and literally screamed.

Oh Tannenbaum, that was awesome!

Adasser pulled out of me before releasing his load, his cock a stone pillar. Nestor picked up the icicle and pushed it in and out of me, while Santa once again rocked the swing. The cold did little to douse my ardor. If anything, it only increased. Or maybe it was the anticipation. Whichever it was, I knew they were building me up toward another monumental orgasm.

The swing picked up speed again and I lifted my head to find Nestor screwing me, his rock hard dick thrusting in and out of me with a ferocity that bordered on obsession. The vibrating bullet squared up with my clit, which was so majorly stimulated I came embarrassingly quick, squealing like a stuck reindeer. Nestor smirked as he pulled out his cock without coming. He winked at me as he moved back to let Goldir step between my spread thighs. The ice. Ho ho ho, the ice. I was going to have to try this trick with my vibrator when I got home.

Santa rocked me gently into the icicle. By now I was on to their tricks and found it difficult to remain unaffected by what I knew was in store for me. Those cock cages were magic, turning their dicks into orgasm granting missiles. Goldir's member was by far the thickest and the shortest, which meant that the vibrating nub would hit me faster than it had with the others. This was going to be some ride.

Goldir drove into me without warning, taking control of the swing from Santa. I was frantic as took everything he was giving me. Gasping, I tried to resist coming, but the force of him was too strong. Before I knew it, I screamed in ecstasy, my voice hoarse. I was surely ruined for all other men. My guys had spoiled me to the point where I thought I'd died if I came again.

One more. I had to take one more.

I flopped back into the swing, letting it carry me back and forth the way the wind sweeps a snowbank. I was a ragdoll. Limp. The chains continued their assault. I still wasn't used to the sensations they elicited. Each tug was a surprise and kept me constantly off kilter. That was the sexiest thing—not knowing what was coming. I surely never expected what Santa did next.

The speakers belted out I'll Be Home for Christmas as Santa flipped me over onto my stomach in the swing. Somehow my torso was supported while the chains continued to swing free. In this position the pull was deeper and much more erotic. I groaned at the carnal onslaught. The swing was adjusted so that my ass stuck up higher in the air. I felt a pressure on my anal rose, then the slide of something thick and...pepperminty? I turned to see Santa driving a glass candy cane coated in what must be peppermint scented lube into my ass. The tingle from the mint was exquisite.

I strained back, wanting it in all the way up to the curve. Santa twisted it so that the handle was out of the way. Nestor had taken Santa's place controlling the swing and he set it into a gentle rock. This time the icicle felt different—both hot *and* cold. He must've coated it with the peppermint lube. Holly jolly Christmas to me!

Nestor's face was level to mine so he got to see the expressions crossing my face. He gazed back at me with something close to admiration and lust. Lots and lots of lust. This elf wanted me. And not just for tonight. I found myself drowning in the magical pools of his eyes and what I saw there made me feel both sexy and cherished. For the first time I wondered what it would be like to know him in the real world, outside my fantasy. Was I someone he might want?

The dual sensations of hot and cold in my pussy and hot in my ass combined with the look on Nestor's face shot me toward orgasm. Just as I was about to come, Santa withdrew the icicle. I gasped, hanging on the edge. One corner of Nestor's lips kicked up. He *liked* seeing me denied. What would that fantasy be like? I suddenly wondered. Tonight was all about me getting some...no, it was about me getting it *all*. But what would it be like if I had one man who made me wait...and wait...and *wait* to come?

Nestor could be that lover. I could see it in his eyes. He was handsome and he clearly liked me. A lot. I wished there was some way I could get to know him outside this fantasy. But that was against the rules. It was all about anonymity and matching up fantasies. This wasn't just my sexcapade. It was the guys' fantasy as well. They all wanted this. They'd all paid just as I had for this sexual adventure. We'd been given these roles and this script to play out.

Nestor suddenly pushed the swing back and let go. Because of the numbing of the ice I didn't feel Santa until he was fully seated in my pussy. He was driving this sleigh now. And oh, what a ride! With each hard thrust I swore he got deeper and deeper. The clit vibe that the elves had worn on top was on the bottom of Santa's cock cage so that I got that extra shock with every lunge. He was brutal and I loved it.

Nestor watched me swing back and forth while stroking his swollen un-caged cock. He liked seeing me get reamed by another man. He liked to watch. My stars, he was perfect for me. Where would I meet another man who not only embraced my curves, he luxuriated in them? Where would I find a guy who liked the same kink I did and who was so into Christmas that he *wanted* to dress up like an elf even though a lot of little people found the thought rather insulting?

I was going to come and it was going to be a doozy. Between the candy cane in my ass, the peppermint lube, the chains, Santa's relentless thrusts and Nestor watching me I was lost in a sexual haze.

"I'm coming!" I shouted right before it crashed into me, ending my exclamation on a loud moan that felt like it was ripped from my very soul.

My pussy pulsed in wave after wave of bliss. The orgasm just kept coming. I couldn't catch my breath and suddenly everything went black. I woke up what must've been seconds later to find myself on the ground surrounded by four very hot, very concerned men.

"I'm all right," I told them.

Goldir checked my pulse like a pro. Could he be a nurse or doctor in real life? "Her heart rate is elevated," he announced, his voice much deeper than I'd anticipated, and I realized I hadn't heard him speak this entire time. "But otherwise she's okay. How are you feeling, babe?" he asked me.

"Like I just had the most incredible orgasm of my life," I answered. "I think you guys might have ruined me for anyone else."

All four of them chuckled.

"I've never come so hard in all my life," Adasser admitted shyly.

"Me neither," Nestor chimed in, his voice so deep it made my clit pulse with new life. "I think your pussy might have ruined me for all others."

"You have the sweetest cunt," Santa agreed. "I could stay buried in it for days."

Goldir nodded. "It hooks me and just won't let go until I'm milked dry. Think you might be up for one more round? We still have time and my dick has never been harder." He gave it a rough stroke. "I need to come, babe, and I want to come all over your gorgeous tits."

There were nods all around. How could I resist?

"Well then," I purred. "Let's take control of this adventure." I arched my back, drawing my arms above my head to make my breasts more inviting. "I'm all yours, boys."

CHAPTER 6

They led me to a new room. It was INCREDIBLE. I gasped when I entered, clasping a hand to my bare chest. Never in my wildest fantasies had I ever imagined a room more beautiful than this. It was like they took the inside of my head and everything I loved about Christmas and made it into a room. Lights twinkled everywhere, reflecting off walls painted a deep forest green. Inset into the walls were jewels that glowed and moved like ornaments on a tree. The ceiling was a star, the perfect tree topper.

There was no furniture, only cushions...no, pillows...no, *boughs*. Soft swaying boughs. The light scent of pine served to enhance the visual imagery. It was like being *inside* a Christmas tree. That's the only way to describe it. I could hardly breathe, it was so beautiful. My guys seemed to be as stunned as I was by the grandeur, their wide gazes roaming the room. This was clearly the first time they were seeing it too. Everything up until now had been carefully choreographed. The room was as much their surprise as it was mine. O Tannenbaum played gently, adding to the atmosphere.

The five of us glanced at each other questioningly. No one seemed to know what to do. Their dicks were still impressively hard. I needed to do something about that. But what? We'd already done just about everything I could think of and probably everything they could think of. What did that leave?

"Well," I started, "what do you guys want to do?"

"Fuck you," Goldir said bluntly. "Fuck your cunt and your tits. Come on your chest."

"Okay. You got it. What about you, Adasser?" I asked.

He looked a little shy about telling me what he wanted so I gave him an encouraging smile.

"I like your ass," he finally said.

"An ass man. I like it." I winked. "My ass is yours. Nestor?"

"I want to be on top of you," he answered. "Missionary."

Why that gave me an extra flutter I don't know. Usually plain old vanilla sex didn't do it for me, but the look in Nestor's eyes told me that it was going to be anything *but* ordinary.

"I'd like that," I told him. "Santa?"

"I want to eat your pussy, then have you to suck me off," he said, like he was ordering dinner. "With a finger in my ass. Maybe two."

Well then. "Two fingers it is. What order are we doing this in, gentlemen?"

The guys got together and started a game of rock, paper, scissors. After a few tries where no one won I put my fingers in my mouth and whistled to get their attention.

"How about we go in alphabetical order?" I suggested.

They all nodded. Adasser stepped toward me. The other

guys got comfortable across the room to watch, stroking their cocks in anticipation of the show. It was no surprise that Adasser wanted my ass. After all, ass was in his name.

I lay down on the cushions, wondering how he wanted to do this. Until now, all of the decisions had been made for us. Every exquisite detail of tonight had been choreographed for us as we'd requested when signing up for this adventure so there was some awkwardness as Adasser lay down next to me. As soon as he kissed me, all of my unease went away. It was just he and I in this beautiful room. All we had to do was pleasure each other. That shouldn't be too difficult, right?

He was an intense kisser, pouring everything he had into it. I could feel him, the essence of him, through his kiss. He was a good man, if a bit shy. But I liked that about him because underneath was a man of great strength. He gave me his total focus. There was no doubt at all that he was into me and into me good. My thick waist and heavy thighs were a turnon to him. More than once he grabbed a handful and growled, coming at me with renewed passion.

Adasser was a thorough lover. By the time he rolled me to my stomach and lubed up his cock, I was panting in expectation. I couldn't wait for him to drive his cock into my ass and give it a good reaming. He gripped my hips, kneading his hands in my flesh as though imprinting himself on me. Pushing me down flat on the pillows, he widened my legs as far as they would go. His cock was built for this, long and a bit narrow, especially at the tip. I quivered in anticipation.

His lubed finger rimmed my ass before sliding in. He hooked his finger, stroking my g-spot from the other side. I moaned. It felt so good. He knew what he was doing. A second and then a third finger soon joined the first. He stretched me tenderly and thoroughly. I begged for his cock. I wanted it so bad. Every time I stuck my butt in the air he pushed it back down and gave it a smack that only intensified my expectation. He withdrew his fingers and I knew this was it. I held still, anxious for that first punch past my anal ring.

His cock slipped in with little pressure. I moaned as my body drew him deeper with each push until he was fully seated. It took everything in me not to move. He held me down and withdrew slowly. The slow scrape of his cock made me whimper. He soon found his rhythm, setting a gentle, leisurely pace, lolling me into the false sense that this would be an unhurried coupling. O Christmas tree, was I wrong.

His thrusts grew steadily more rapid until I had to hold on or get pushed across the pillows. He was relentless, the drag and lunge so constant I had a hard time keeping up. I was wild, screaming my head off in pleasure as my orgasm hit. He drove hard into me, shooting his hot cum deep. He collapsed on top of me, his head resting on the small of my back as he fought as hard as I did to catch my breath. He turned his head and licked the dent where my ass met my waist. I shuddered, my clit pulsing and aching so bad that I ground it into the pillows to get some relief.

He slid out of me and kissed my giant globes, first one then the other, finishing with a sharp slap that made me yelp then grin. I rolled over. He fondled my breast almost absently as he kissed me.

"You have the hottest ass," he whispered in my ear. "I could fuck it everyday and never be satisfied. If you want me, I'm yours. Whenever you want." He winked at me, then kissed the breast he'd been playing with before sauntering off across the room and sitting down with a smug look on his face.

Was there anything sexier than a confident, well pleasured man?

Goldir rose to his feet and approached me, his thick cock bobbing up and down. His gaze was glued to my chest. Definitely a boob man the way Adasser was an ass man. Lucky for me I was all about the cock since I had four gorgeous ones at my disposal. I was looking forward to Goldir's and the way he held no pretense, shoving into me with little to no fanfare. He was all *Here's my cock, take it, take aalllll of it.*

Playing with my nipples (which he seemed to *really* like), I widened my legs for him, exposing my nearly hairless cunt. His gaze bounced between my crotch and my tits like a kid in a candy store trying to choose his favorite. He shoved a pillow beneath my ass until he got me exactly where he wanted me. Kneeling between my thighs, he rubbed the blunt head of his cock through my slickness. Without warning, he thrust into me. The shock of it made me gasp in a good way. I pinched my nipples harder, rolling them between my fingers and arching my back to take him at the best possible angle.

He filled me completely. There was almost no room for him to move, but that didn't stop him. Gripping my legs for purchase, he came at me hard, pounding into me. His thumb strummed my desperate clit and in no time at all, I came. He rode me through it. As soon as I crested he pulled out, pushed my legs down, and straddled me.

Grabbing my boobs, he made a nest for his cock, still wet from my pussy, and thrust between my giant mounds. He shouted when he came, shooting his steaming cum on my neck and chest. It seemed to go on forever. His cock milk ran down my shoulders. I swiped a finger through it and sucked on it. His eyes widened and his dick pulsed out a final squirt that hit me on the chin. I licked it up like ice cream. His jizz tasted fantastic.

He kissed me open-mouthed just as aggressive and unapologetic as he fucked. I gripped his head, holding him to me as we mashed his cum between us. Messy sex was the *best* sex.

He cradled my tits in his hands. "These are so fucking hot with my cum on them," he said. "Any time you want a pearl necklace you call me." He thrust his tongue in my mouth one more time before climbing off me and joining the other guys across the room.

I left Goldir's jizz on me. It was erotic. Like he'd marked me or something.

Nestor rose to his feet and came toward me like a man on a mission. Out of all of them I connected with him the most. There was something about this sexy elf that jingled all of my bells. His cock bounced as we walked. He wasn't the biggest and he wasn't the smallest. He was just right. For me anyway. I couldn't wait to find out what he had in store for me.

He removed the pillow from under my ass, laying me out flat. And then he just stood there over me. The look in his eyes should've scorched, but there was something else there too. Something that looked and felt a lot like affection. He circled me. There wasn't an inch of my body he hadn't already seen, but gazed at me as though seeing me for the first time. My first instinct was to put my hands up and cover myself. He saw too much, more than just my skin.

I wanted to tell him to get on with the banging already, but he wasn't to be rushed. He lay down next to me and put his arms around me. There was something careful and purposeful about the embrace and nothing at all sexual about it, which threw me off guard. That's why we were all here. To fuck. Not him.

When he put his lips to mine I melted as though this was my very first kiss. He held my face as he kissed me. His tongue swept past my lips. I opened for him. He tasted of mint and smelled like sex. His body pressed to mine felt right, like we were a matched set. Even though we didn't line up the usual way because of his height, we fit. There's no other way to put it.

He pulled back and gazed into my eyes. I smiled and he smiled back.

"Hi, beautiful," he said.

"Hi, handsome."

His thumb smoothed along my jawline. Even though we weren't alone it felt like it was just the two of us in this room. Everything else melted away. He trailed a line of kisses down my neck. I arched into him, giving him better access. This wasn't going to be a mad coupling. No. He was going to take his time with me. I shivered as he brushed his hand over my nipple, then cupped my large breast. I was more than a handful, more than two handfuls. His mouth moved across my skin, creating a burning path.

I ran my hands over his body, mapping the layout. I loved the way his ass curved out from his back so forthright and proud. I gripped it in both hands as he wedged his leg against my pussy. His mouth found my breast and he drew my nipple deep into his mouth. His other hand was busy at my other breast. I writhed under him. This man knew what he was doing. It was a slow buildup. Anticipation mingled with desire into a heady brew and I was drunk off it.

His mouth and hands were magic. My body was on fire for him. He made his way down my body, kissing and licking a path that left me panting. He entered me slowly.

My pussy adjusted to accommodate him, closing around
him. His cock was a perfect fit almost as though we were
made for each other. He moved in and out of me slowly,
building the pleasure like a great architect. There was
nothing plain or vanilla about this. It was everything. He
was everything. His mouth closed over my nipple and I
gasped. I was *so* close.

His rhythm increased. I was swept away on a tide of
whispered praise mixed with the slap of flesh on flesh. He
worked over me, taking me higher and higher until I broke,
coming on a choked sob. It was beautiful. He was beautiful
as he ground hard against me and spent himself inside me.
He sagged on top of me. The weight of him felt good and I
imagined more times like this with him, our bodies as close
as two people can get. I wanted this. I wanted *him*.

He pulled out of me and crawled up my body. I melted
into his kiss, giving over to the feelings I was beginning to
have for him.

"I'm yours if you want me," he whispered against my
lips. "I don't mind sharing sometimes. I like to watch. I especially like to watch you."

I caressed his hair back from his face. "You truly
wouldn't mind?"

"If you were mine—really mine—I'd want you to be
happy. And the truth is I get off on seeing you with other
guys, watching you come. You're sexy as hell, Marla."

He whispered my name, breaking the rules. We weren't
supposed to use our real names. It went against the guide-
lines of the fantasy. My surprise must've shown on my face
because he did the most extraordinary thing.

"I'm Neil."

I smiled up at him. "Hi, Neil."

He grinned back and he was even more handsome than

ever. "Hi, Marla." He gave me a quick, hard kiss. "My turn's over. I better go."

"Wait." I stopped him before he climbed off me. "Will I see you after this?"

He winked. "Maybe." And then he was gone.

I closed my eyes, going over everything he'd told me and what Goldir and Adasser had said. Could it be? Could they possibly want to take this fantasy into reality? Was that even possible? How would we work that out in the real world?

Santa pressed the long length of his body against mine, trailing a hand up and down my curves. He licked the shell of my ear and I shivered. He was all about the oral. I loved oral. Both giving and receiving. I missed the feel of Nestor— no, Neil—on top of me, but I was heavily anticipating what Santa might do to me. He kissed me deeply and I got the first hint of how it was going to be to have his mouth on my pussy. Insane. The man had a magic tongue. Not only that, he knew how to use his whole mouth, including his teeth and lips.

It wasn't long before I was squirming under him, anxious for the feel of his mouth down south. As if reading my thoughts he sucked, kissed and licked his way down my body until he got to the main show. Moving between my thighs, he parted my legs, opening me up to him. He stared at my pussy for a long time, then licked his lips. An illicit thrill raced up my spine. He grabbed a pillow and propped my ass on it. He nodded, seemingly satisfied with my position and then got down to it.

Pointing his tongue, he licked around my clit, swirling the tight bud. He started slow as if he had all night. That laziness was my undoing. I relaxed back and let him take me where he wanted. Where we went was a one-way ticket to pleasure town. Easing two fingers into me, he stroked my inner wall right over my g-spot. He was a maestro, playing me like a Stradivarius. He took me to heights I didn't realize I could go.

He changed the angle and tempo of his tongue, using it to vibrate against my clit. My inner walls shook with the beginnings of my orgasm. I thrashed my head on the pillows, almost fighting against the inevitable. A third finger joined the fun, then a fourth, filling me completely. I arched into his hand and mouth, clamping a hand on his head to keep him right where I wanted him. Bliss. Nirvana. Fireworks. The whole shebang. He drew it out and then clamped his mouth down on my clit and sucked. I *lost* it.

He rode me through it, holding me down so he could draw out my climax to the max. I don't know how long it went on but I'm pretty sure I celebrated a birthday and every other holiday in the year. I came down to find Santa grinning at me over the top of my mound, his face wet with my juices. That had to be the most erotic sight I'd ever seen. I trembled in the aftermath, not sure I'd ever be the same. No one had ever eaten me out like that before. I doubted they ever would again. Santa brought me the best present.

He gave me a hard smacking kiss, transferring some of my wetness to my lips. I licked them, tasting myself. That seemed to have a galvanizing effect on Santa. His cock jerked and dripped on my belly.

"Not yet," I told him, taking hold of his cock and squeezing. "You're coming in my mouth. I can't wait to taste you."

He groaned and flopped down beside me, his arms and legs splayed. He was all mine to do whatever I wanted with. And what I wanted was his cock in my mouth. It was my turn to move between his legs, spreading them wide. I found a handy bottle of lube and squirted some on my fingers. He followed my motions, letting out a sound somewhere between agony and ecstasy when he saw that I'd lubed all four of my fingers.

He tipped his head back as I took hold of his cock. It was beautifully formed and leaned just a tad to the left. I licked him from his balls to just under the head of his cock, then swirled my tongue under the lip, applying a little extra pressure to the V. Several drops of pre-cum bubbled up. I ignored it despite dying for a taste of him, continuing my slow torture. He gripped the pillows in his fists as I slipped a finger past his anal ring. With my first swipe across his p-spot his hips flexed and he let out a low, primal moan.

I glanced at my men across the room. All three of their cocks were hard and ready. They *liked* watching me pleasure another man. I liked showing them what I could do. They jerked on their dicks, masturbating to the show before them. There wasn't any sexier sight in the world.

I redoubled my efforts on Santa's cock. It was long and thickly veined and as hard as a diamond. I was going to make this so good for him and the other guys watching. They'd talk about this night, this coupling years from now. I swiped my tongue across his cum slit, sighing as I finally got a taste of him. Delicious. I couldn't wait to have his hot jizz shoot down my throat. I pulled my finger out of his ass and added a second one. His head and heels dug into the pillows. The sound he made caused my pussy to drip. So *hot*.

I took his cock fully into my mouth, experimenting with how far he could go. I opened the back of my throat and sucked hard, drawing him deep. He groaned, his hips lifting and helping me do the job. I worked a third finger into his ass and I thought he was going to lose it with the noise he made. An answering echo came from my guys across the room. They were living vicariously through Santa. Good. I'd do them all like this, I vowed, knowing it probably would never be.

By the time I slid my fourth finger past his anal ring, he was inconsolable. I stroked him inside, while sucking him down like a Hoover. His hips jerked and his hot cum shot into my mouth, filling it. His hoarse cry reverberated around the room. All four of my guys came at once. Shooting their loads, their gazes boring into me. Never had I known such satisfaction in pleasuring a man. No. *Men*. I'd managed to get them all off at the same time.

I pulled my fingers out of Santa's ass and my mouth off his cock. Finding hand wipes close by, I cleaned my fingers, then climbed up Santa's body to kiss him. He grabbed me roughly, rolling so that I was under him.

"Your mouth is incredible," he whispered roughly. "And your cunt..." He sighed. "Unbelievable. I have to have you again."

"I'd like that, but I don't know if it's possible."

He nodded. "I know. The damn rules."

Just then, chimes went off and the lights flickered.

It was over.

CHAPTER 7

The rest of the weekend drug by slowly. I was sore from my sexcapade, but I had no regrets. It was *exactly* what I'd wanted. I only wished I could've kept my guys. I got something from each of them that I didn't want to give up.

I walked into the lobby of my office building in downtown Chicago Monday morning a little bow-legged and more satisfied than I'd ever felt in my life. I waved at the security guard as I strode to the bank of elevators. I'd taken extra care with my hair, makeup, and wardrobe that morning, wanting to appear as sexy and satisfied as I felt. The guard did a double take. He'd only ever gone as far as a friendly wave before. This time he took me in from head to toe and back again.

By the time he finished I was a little moist in the panties and watched with a sly smile as he adjusted his junk. I winked at him and his mouth fell open. I guess there was something to the saying that the sexiest thing a woman can wear is confidence.

I joined the queue waiting for the elevator. There was

quite a crowd this morning. In front of me was a tall man with white hair. Probably a partner in one of the firms in the building. I didn't pay much attention to the big wigs. I was a lowly secretary to a CEO, not exactly making the big bucks. My weekend extravagance had set me back quite a bit *and* used up all of my savings. But it was worth it. I smiled just thinking about it. A man in a suit next to me gave me the once over. I batted my eyelashes at him, then looked away like I didn't care about him. Who was this woman who openly flirted with strangers, meeting their gazes and not caring what they thought?

It looked like the weekend had changed more than my financial situation.

The doors of the elevator opened and everyone crowded in. I managed to muscle my way in. Just before the doors closed a man stuck his hand between them and they reopened. Someone in the back complained. I rolled my eyes, then sucked in a breath at the sight of Goldir entering the elevator car. *What was he doing here?*

He acted as though he had no idea who I was, just like he was supposed to. I stared down at his head in front of me, remembering the feel of his thick cock inside me. My nipples puckered and I tugged my sweater closed to hide them. *Did he not recognize me?* You'd think you'd remember someone you'd screwed six ways to Sunday and back. The car stopped on a floor and we all shuffled around to let whoever had pressed the button off. I got shoved off to the side as we readjusted so I couldn't see the person who entered the car.

The elevator resumed its climb, stopping on four more floors. My office was near the top. I had to factor into my morning routine the time it took to get to my floor on top of the time it took just to get to my building. I was going to be late at this rate. I hadn't taken all these stops into consideration. More people came and went and I got stuffed into a corner next to Goldir. *Should I say something? What would I say?* That was a great fuck fest, wasn't it? Are you as sore as I am?

No. That wouldn't do.

I could ask him if he knew Nestor...I mean Neil. Maybe he had his number.

I tapped him on the shoulder. "Excuse me."

He glanced up at me his face blank. "Yes?" No recognition.

Now what?

"You look very familiar," I said. "Have we met?"

He looked me up and down. "I'd remember if we did."

"So would I," a man I couldn't see in the other corner said.

I strained to spot him with no luck. The doors opened again and there was more shifting. Goldir disappeared. I ended up with a man with a serious hard-on behind me. He brushed me with it before I moved away. I made a face. *Why did guys think that was okay to do?*

On the floor before mine, the elevator emptied except for Goldir, boner man, and me. I kept my eyes on the number above the door. The elevator passed my floor.

"Damn it." I hit the button, but it just kept going.

I'd have to go to the top floor and then come back down. I was going to be late. Double damn it!

The car went all the way to the top floor. When the doors opened I sucked in a breath and took a step back right into boner man who gripped my arms. I looked up at him—Santa—then back at Nestor (no...Neil) and Adasser entering the elevator. I didn't know what to do. I was too shocked to move, my feet stuck to the floor. As soon as the door closed Neil hit the emergency button, keeping us from moving.

"W-w-what's going on?" I gasped.

Neil stepped toward me. He was sharply dressed, as were my other guys, in a three-piece suit and tie. *Very* sexy.

"That's Greg." Neil gestured toward Goldir, then to Adasser, then Santa. "And that's Adam and Sam. We have a proposition for you we're hoping you'll consider. We went through a lot of trouble to find you and set this up. We're hoping you'll say yes." He glanced at the other guys. "They're as hot for you as I am." They each nodded in turn. Neil took my hand. "But they're not looking for anything permanent. *I* am."

I didn't know what to say.

Adasser...*Adam* took my other hand. Santa...no, *Sam's* arms came around me from behind. Greg or Goldir leaned against the wall of the car, giving me a look like he knew exactly what I had up my skirt. And damned if he didn't.

"I'm n-n-not sure what you want from me," I stammered, enjoying the feeling of having my guys all around me again.

"We want to fuck you when we want to fuck you," Sam whispered in my ear. "No strings attached. Neil wants more than that, but he's willing to share. He *likes* to share."

Neil nodded.

"H-h-how exactly would this work?" I asked.

Greg adjusted his cock through his pants. "We call you when we're in the mood. You let us know if you're in the mood. Or you can call us. If it works out there's a fuck fest. If not, we try another night."

"I'm not s-s-sure I could do a repeat of the other night every weekend," I told them. "I'm awfully sore from what we did."

Each of them got equally smug grins on their faces.

They'd reamed me pretty good and they knew it. Smug bastards.

"Take us one at a time," Neil said. "Or two at a time. Or three. Whatever you want. You call the shots. Where, when, how often, and with whom. All your call. You know our specialties, what we'd bring to the occasion."

"So you're saying I could order you up like takeout food?" I asked, incredulous.

"That's exactly what we're saying," Adam said softly. It was hard to believe this shy man could pound ass like an Olympic champion.

I turned to Neil. "You said you were looking for something permanent. What does that mean and how would this little...arrangement work into that?"

"I want to take you out. Meet your friends. You meet mine. The usual. We'd be exclusive. Except for these guys. And I'd *always* get to watch."

"Even if you're not participating?"

"Even then."

"I don't know what to say..."

Sam gave me a squeeze. "Say yes. I can't stop thinking about the taste of your pussy and the way you sucked my cock. I want you again. And again. And again."

"And you're all okay with this?" I asked them.

Another chorus of nods. Was *I* okay with this? A fantasy was one thing. Reality was quite another. As I glanced around at my guys I decided that I was more than okay with it. I wanted it. No. I *craved* it. There was just one little thing to settle.

"What happens when you meet someone else? What happens if I want to call it quits?"

"Then it's over," Sam said. "Maybe one of us will drop out at a time. Maybe two will. Who knows? We just want to keep it going for as long as it lasts, as long as you'll have us."

"What do you say?" Greg asked.

I took a deep breath and let it out slowly. "I say *Merry Christmas* to me."

PIANO LESSONS

LESSON 1

I met Johnny Miller at a USO square dance in January 1943 at the University of Colorado, where he was visiting family before heading off to war. He spent all evening dancing in my square. At the end of the night he kissed me. Three weeks later, we ran off to California together and got married.

My father, Joseph Q. Feldon, of Feldon's department stores, swore he'd never speak to me again. He stayed true to his word, permanently cutting me off financially. My brother and sister would inherit the department store empire. I was out of the will.

I didn't care. I was in love.

Six months after we got married, Johnny shipped out. I was left alone in California. I started teaching piano to a few of the neighborhood children for some extra money and to pass the time until the war was over and my Johnny came home.

Those were lonely months. The loneliest months of my life. I was a nineteen-year-old war wife, doing my part for our boys abroad. Once a week I treated myself to a movie.

The newsreels were full of images of our men, fighting for freedom. I looked and looked, hoping to get a glimpse of my Johnny. I never saw him.

Once a week I'd get a letter from him. He always addressed them the same: To my Ruby Rose, and they were full of how much he missed and loved me. I wrote him three letters a week faithfully, sometimes sending along a snapshot of me. I didn't want him to forget what I looked like. If I closed my eyes I could still hear his voice, but as the weeks turned to months, I stopped hearing his voice as clearly and couldn't remember the way his arms felt around me.

And then the telegram came.

Dear Mrs. Miller,

It is our sad obligation to report that Private Jonathon Petre Miller was killed in action.

I was a widow at nineteen.

My first thought was to call my parents. I wanted to go home. But Daddy had been adamant that I was on my own. Without the money Johnny sent me, times got tough. I barely scrapped by on the money I made giving piano lessons. I managed to get a part-time job—ironically, at Feldon's department store. It was all I could find. If it weren't for the tiny house in Long Beach that Johnny had inherited from his grandmother, I would've been out on the street.

It was hard keeping up the old house. Things broke all the time. The kitchen faucet busted off in my hand, spraying water everywhere. Frantic, I called the first plumber in the phone book. By the time he showed up, the kitchen was flooded and I was in tears, sweeping water out the back door to keep it from spreading to the rest of the house.

He was a big swarthy man, the plumber, with deep-set eyes and arms full of tattoos. He introduced himself as Aaron of Aaron's Plumbing. He frightened me a little, reminding me of the toughs who used to make comments as my friends and I walked by back in Colorado.

Thankfully, Aaron got the water shut off right away, stopping the flood. I leaned on the broom and watched him work, dread pooling in my belly. I didn't have much money left after my trip to the grocery store this morning.

He didn't talk much. Lots of grunts and short sentences. But he was efficient, finishing the job in just under an hour. When he was done, he rubbed his dark-whiskered jaw. "That'll be eight eighty-five, including parts."

I stared at him in shock. I didn't have the money. "Would you take payments?"

"Payment in full only."

"Trade then?"

His dark gaze slid over me. "For what?"

"I teach piano. Perhaps your children—"

"Don't got any."

"Your wife then."

"Don't got one of them either." He wiped his hands on a rag, regarding me with interest. "What else you got to trade?"

Nothing. I had nothing. Except...

I fingered the locket around my neck that Johnny had given me with his photo in it before shipping out. It was all I had. I undid the clasp and held it out to Aaron. "Would you take this?"

He stepped closer, his gate disjointed. I'd noticed he moved funny while he worked, using the counter to push himself up off the floor. He was close enough that I could smell the spice of his cologne and the tang of his sweat. It had been months since I'd been this close to a man.

I suddenly missed my Johnny something terrible, and the feel of his body close to mine. The loneliness crept over me like a fog and I had to bite the inside of my cheek to keep from crying.

"Pretty bauble," he said.

"My husband gave it to me."

"Where's your husband?"

"Killed in action."

"Sorry." He curled his fingers around mine, closing my hand with the locket inside. "You keep it."

His eyes were full of sorrow. He was being kind to me when he didn't have to. I felt bad for thinking the things I'd thought about him. His large hand was warm and strong and sure over mine. My Johnny's hands had been like that—possessive, reassuring. A fierce longing swept over me, making me sway toward him. It had been too long since I'd been touched. Not even so much as a hug since my Johnny had left me. What it would be like to have *this* man's hands on me, on my body. Would he be big *all over*?

"Is there something...something else I have that you might want?" My voice was breathy, my heart beating like a conga drum. I edged a little closer, until our hands were the only thing between our bodies. "Is there some...*other* way I could pay you?"

I couldn't believe what I was proposing. It took him a moment to get my meaning. When he did his eyes widened. My nipples went rigid against the wet front of my dress, despite the warm day. I'd only ever been with my Johnny, and it had been good. He'd made me feel sensual and desirable. I think I missed that most of all, that look he'd give me. The same look Aaron was giving me now.

"Some *other* way?" he asked, his voice hoarse.

"I'm lonely," I whispered desperately. "I don't have any money to pay you. I don't have anything to trade. I don't have anything of value you might want. All I have is me."

"What if all I want is *you*?"

"What would it take to pay off the debt?"

"How much do you charge for those piano lessons?"

"Thirty cents an hour."

He nodded sadly. "I charge fifty cents an hour."

"I'd pay my hourly rate against the bill." I swallowed hard. "However you want."

"What if I just want you to touch me?"

I put a hand on his chest. His skin was hot under the rough cotton of his shirt, his muscles hard. "Like this?"

He grunted.

"Shirt on or off."

"Off."

I worked the buttons of his shirt until it parted. He sucked in a breath as I smoothed it back and off his shoulders. The shirt hit the ground and all I could see was the wide expanse of his chest. More tattoos. My Johnny hadn't had any tattoos. He didn't believe in them.

The thought of my husband brought a fresh pang of sorrow and loneliness, but surprisingly no guilt.

Aaron took me by the wrists and put my hands on his bare chest. He groaned and closed his eyes as I touched him. The tattoos camouflaged scars, I realized. Lots of scars. His breath grew rough, his chest rising and falling rapidly. The front of his trousers bulged. He did nothing but sway while he stood there and let me touch him.

"Would you like... That is, would you be more comfortable lying down?"

He opened his slumberous eyes and looked down at me. "Where?"

I took his hand and led him to my bedroom. The quilt I'd made from scraps of my Johnny's old shirts covered the bed. I peeled it back and motioned for Aaron to lie down.

He sat on the edge of the bed and removed his boots, then he stood and hooked his thumbs into the waist of his pants with a question in his eyes.

I nodded for him to go ahead. I'd seen a man before. Aaron's maleness wouldn't bother me. I actually grew flush at the thought.

"I was in an accident," he told me in way of warning. "I lost a leg. I have scars."

I ran a finger over a nasty one on his chest just over his heart. "Like this one?"

He nodded gruffly. "You aren't put off?"

"Me? No. My granny used to say that scars are proof we fought hard and won." To prove it, I brushed his hands aside and unfastened his trousers. His member was hard and large. I froze in fascination to stare at it pressing against his underpants.

"You don't got to do nothing with that. Our deal was for touching." He made to refasten his trousers, but I held on firmly.

"What if I want...?" I licked my lower lip. "That is, if you want, I could touch you there too."

"I haven't been touched there like that since the accident."

"How long?"

"Eight years. No woman wants half a man."

"We have a bargain, don't we?"

"For touching."

"Yeah," I said softly. "For touching."

I pulled his trousers and underpants down his hips. His giant cock sprang free. I had to lean to the side to keep it out of my face as I pushed his pants the rest of the way down.

His body looked like a war zone. His right leg cruelly cut off above the knee. Or at least where the knee should've been. A crude simulation of a leg was attached to his stump with straps. The skin around it was red and tender looking. Scars of different shapes and thicknesses covered nearly the entire font of his body.

I gave him a little push and he bounced onto the bed.

Bending down, I helped him the rest of the way out of his pants. His whole body shook as though a tornado ripped through it. Don't know if he caught a chill or if it was because I couldn't stop looking and touching. His body fascinated me. There was strength and vulnerability and pain. So much pain.

I reached for the buttons on my dress. I didn't know where my boldness came from. Looking at Aaron's torn-up body made me think of my Johnny and his last moments. He'd suffered badly from his wounds before he'd died, according to the funeral director who'd prepared him for burial. Oh, how many times I wished I could've been there to soothe him and care for him. I wanted to do for Aaron what I couldn't do for Johnny—take away his pain and replace it with pleasure.

Aaron leaned up on his elbows. "What are you doing?"

"Touching you."

He made a low noise in the back of his throat, causing the place between my legs to go slick. I dropped my dress and went to work on my underthings. His eyes never left me. They burned like black coals. When I was nude, I lay down on the bed next to him and pressed my body against his. Oh, that was nice. His body was hairier than Johnny's, but that only made it more masculine.

He didn't touch me at first, lying stiffly next to me. Slowly he relaxed. First one arm snaked around me then the other.

He was a furnace. I imagined *him* warming my bed at

night instead of the hot water bottle I normally used. I'd forgotten how good it was to have a man in my bed.

Sifting my fingers through the hair on his chest, I grew bolder, sliding my hand down his hard, marred stomach. He didn't stop me like I expected him to. The hairs around his member were springy and wiry and dark, black as night. His manhood dripped stickiness that mixed with his hairs, turning them white. I ran an experimental finger through the wetness. His chest rumbled beneath my head and his member leaked more fluid as I licked my finger.

I'd tasted my Johnny many times. He'd taught me how to take him in my mouth and to use my hands on him. He'd put his mouth on me too. It had taken me a while to get used to that. Good girls didn't do those things. The more comfortable I became, the bolder my Johnny got, until we were doing things I was sure would send me straight to hell. The only thing was—I'd liked it. A lot. My Johnny made me feel beautiful and cherished. I could be brazen and out of control with him. The wilder I became, the more my Johnny had praised me. Oh, how I *missed* his adoration.

And I missed having a man inside me. I missed the touch of a man and his weight on top of me. I missed being taken from behind. I missed the touching, the kissing, the licking, the sticky wetness between my legs. I missed the way my body shook with pleasure.

Aaron didn't say anything or make any move to stop me from taking him in my mouth. The only movement he made was a subtle thrusting of his hips off the bed. He was large, much larger than my Johnny had been. It took me a little while to figure out how to handle him. He required both of my hands and even when I had him at the back of my throat, I couldn't get to all of him.

A tentative, gentle hand moved up my back and cradled

my head. His good leg shifted restless over the bunched-up covers, kicking them onto the floor. The heady musk of his sex filled my nose, making me wetter between the legs.

He flexed his fingers in my hair. "Mrs. Miller," he murmured. "Mrs. Miller, I can't stop."

I sucked him as far back as I could and massaged his sack. He thrashed and groaned. He pulled my hair. My mouth suddenly filled with his seed. Torrents of it. I gulped it down greedily, as my Johnny had taught me. Aaron tasted different. Good, but different. I licked him until he grew flaccid in my hand and his breathing slowed.

He pulled me onto him and kissed the top of my head. "Thank you, Mrs. Miller."

"Don't call me Mrs. Miller. It's Ruby. Call me Ruby."

LESSON 2

I paid off Aaron in three sessions, each a week apart. At the end of the last session, while he was still hard inside me, he asked if he could take me out to dinner. I laughed and told him I'd love to, but I didn't need a boyfriend and I wasn't looking for a husband. I needed a job. A steady income.

He proposed something that at first struck me as insane. No. Insulting. My mouth was open to refuse in the most blistering way when it struck me. I'd already been doing what he was suggesting and I hadn't been bothered by it.

He offered to pay me for my time.

Twice the hourly wage he charged for plumbing. That was a whole lot more than I was making at Feldon's and buckets more than I made giving children, who didn't practice, piano lessons. I agreed and we set up the terms. He would come to me every Tuesday at four-thirty in the afternoon. He winked and called it *his* piano lesson.

My Tuesday afternoons with Aaron helped my finances a good deal, but I was still coming up short. The property taxes on the house were due soon and I didn't have the money. If I didn't pay, I'd lose my home. I mentioned my problem to Aaron one afternoon when he caught me staring off into space.

"My husband didn't pay them last year and I owe for this year," I told Aaron. "I could lose the house."

"If I had it to give to you, I would," he said in earnest.

I believed him. He was a good man, a ferocious lover, and a solid presence in my life that I'd come to rely on.

"Maybe you could give *piano lessons* to others like me." His voice was low and cautious, his gaze downcast as he played with a strand of my hair. "Not sure I'd like sharing you though."

I considered his notion. Our arrangement was special. I wasn't sure how I'd even go about doing what he suggested.

"I know a fella," he continued in the same careful manner. "The brother of a friend. Broken like me. Almost died fighting for our country. Been real down. Maybe you could do for him what you've done for me. He could more than afford you."

And that was how I came to meet Jack.

He knocked on my door a week later on Wednesday morning at nine AM sharp. I didn't know what Aaron had told him about our arrangement or what Jack expected from me, but he looked at me with defiance and anger in his eyes, daring me to make a comment.

Jack was broken all right. He was about my age, maybe a little younger, and styled his hair like Errol Flynn's, letting a lock of it fall forward. On Errol it was rakish and dashing. On Jack it was meant to try to camouflage his eye patch. He balanced on one leg with a crutch tucked up under one arm. His good arm. The limbs on his left side were missing. He wasn't scarred like Aaron, but it was clear he'd been very terribly wounded.

"I'm here for my *piano lesson*." He rolled his eyes at the

euphemism Aaron had come up with for what would seem to be my new occupation.

The cut of Jack's jaw and the shape of his mouth reminded me a bit of my Johnny. I melted at the sight of him, which he appeared to take for pity.

"What are you staring at?" he sneered.

"You." I tentatively reached out to smooth the lock of blond hair off his patch.

He jerked back and nearly tumbled down the steps before regaining his balance. "What are you doing?"

"Seeing if your hair feels as soft as it looks."

"I don't want your sympathy. I came here for a fuck." He pushed past me into the house, knocking me into the doorjamb.

I shouldn't have been shocked at his language. He was only telling the truth. But the base crudeness of his words struck a chord deep within me, bringing the sharp pang of shame. I knew I was prostituting myself to him, but he didn't need to make me feel like a whore.

I followed him down the hall to the bedroom, my cheeks hot and tears stinging the backs of my eyes. I found him in the process of stripping off his shirt.

"Put your shirt back on and get out of my house."

He blinked at me in surprise. "I'm here for a *piano lesson*," he annunciated as though I was dim, then shoved his hand in his front pocket and pulled out a stack of bills and waved them at me. "I have money."

"I know what you're here for. If your way of doing this is to insult me in the cruelest manner possible, then get out. I don't want or need money from someone who hurts others to make himself feel better."

His laugh was bitter and filled with irony. "Honey, if it's flowers and sweet talk you want, I'm not your man."

"Politeness and decorum go a lot further than flowers."

"I'm sorry." His gaze dropped to the floor and he sounded genuinely remorseful. "I don't like being touched."

"That's going to make what we propose to do rather difficult then, don't you think?"

A corner of his mouth twisted up into a wry grin. "I suppose so."

"Shall we start over?"

He nodded, looking rather chagrined, and stuffed his money back into his pocket.

I held out my hand. "Hello. I'm Ruby Rose."

"Hello, Ruby Rose." He took my hand. "I'm Jack."

"It's nice to meet you, Jack. Please, call me Ruby."

"Can I ask why a pretty lady like you would have to resort to something like..." He gestured toward the bed. "This?"

"No. You may not. That's a very rude and impertinent question."

"I'd've thought it was a perfectly appropriate question in light of what we intend to do."

I sighed. He was rough around the edges, but he was cute and there was something well-meaning in his question.

"Why would *any* woman do what we're proposing to do?"

"Hey, I get it. I'm not in much of a position to judge considering I'm paying for your time. I guess my real question is why—even for the money—would you want to be with me? I'm not exactly throwing off female advances."

I took a measured step closer, wondering if he realized our hands were still clasped. "I think you're very dashing actually." Raising my hand slowly, I swept aside his lock of hair. "Like Errol Flynn." I lowered my hand to his shoulder and moved closer. "I was right."

He watched me with a wary look on his face. "About what?"

"Your hair is as soft as it looks."

His laugh held no mirth. "You're good. Very good. I almost believed..." He shook his head. "Never mind."

I leaned closer, focusing my attention on his mouth and those lips that reminded me so much of my Johnny's. "Believe, Jack."

He didn't back away when our lips met. His mouth gave under mine and he tilted his head, taking the kiss deeper and tangling his tongue with mine. He wasn't as skilled as my Johnny had been, or as rough yet tender as Aaron. There was sorrow in his kiss, but there was hope too. It tasted like honey, melting on my tongue.

I sifted my fingers through the baby-soft hair at his nape. He groaned into my mouth and became more urgent, more demanding.

His arm banded around me. I don't know if it was for support or so that I could feel his member hard and insistent between us. Maybe it was both. I worked open the buttons of his shirt. It was of a finer material than Aaron's, but then Jack wasn't a workingman like Aaron. Not because of his injuries, no. This man came from nice things and gentile manners. The war had worn the shine off of him and left him pitted and chipped. He didn't fit in my new world and I got the feeling he no longer fit in the world he came from before the war.

Had I not married my Johnny and run off with him, my father might've introduced me to a man just like Jack with matrimony in mind.

Jack grew frustrated in my embrace and pulled away with a curse. He overbalanced and fell onto the bed sideways. His crutch clattered to the floor.

"This isn't going to work," he growled. "It was a stupid idea."

He started to reach for his crutch, but I shoved him onto his back. "This works better on the bed." I hiked up my skirt and straddled him, then started to undo the buttons that ran down the front of my dress.

He watched, his eye wide and focused on the progress my hands made. Beneath me, his member grew harder. I tilted my pelvis, rubbing against him. He let out a low, hungry sound, his fingers digging into my thigh. I let the garment gap open as it would. I didn't have the money for fancy underclothing so I'd taken some notions I had found at the five and dime and sewed them to my brazier and underpants. Aaron had approved, but now I worried that my efforts would seem cheap to Jack. He came from a world of silk and lace—French lingerie, not basic white cotton with stitched-on, inexpensive lace.

I pushed my dress off my shoulders and let it fall. Jack licked his lips, his gaze darting between my breasts and where I straddled him. I unhooked my brazier and tossed it aside. I wasn't well endowed. My breasts were a little on the small side and out of proportion for how wide my hips were. My Johnny had always said that more than a handful was a waste anyway, and Aaron hadn't said anything at all about them, just looked hungrily at them right before he worshiped them with his mouth.

I cupped my meager breasts and pinched my nipples, moaning as though I was enjoying it. I'd done this once before for Aaron, trying to play the coquette. It had worked, and it looked as though it was working for Jack too. He flexed his hips up into me, hitting that sensitive spot. I really did enjoy myself then. Rocking against his stiffened member, I rolled my nipples harder between my fingers and thumbs. The sensations built and I was close to my pleasure when Jack let out a strangled cry and bucked under me.

His face flushed red from his collar to his hairline. "Oh, Jesus. Oh, Jesus." He looked down to the placket of his trousers, where a telltale wet spot bloomed.

I gave him a delighted grin and went to work undoing his trousers. He tried to wave me off, but I captured his hand and put it on my breast.

"Let me taste you," I told him.

He didn't try to stop me after that, but he wouldn't look at me either. Especially after I got him naked from the waist down. His one socked leg hung limply over the side of the bed. My movements had dislodged his hand and he now looked away from me, his gaze fixed somewhere on the other side of the room. He didn't have a prosthetic leg like Aaron. His exposed mid-thigh stump had bright red scars that would eventually fade to pink.

I placed the flat of my palms on his thighs, avoiding his injury, and slid them up to clasp his fading member in both hands.

He lurched upward at my first lick. I was too busy sucking him clean to see, but I knew he watched me. I could feel his gaze on the top of my head. It tingled, tiny pinpricks of knowing sensation. Being young, he quickly rebounded, growing hard once again. He touched the top of my head, drawing my attention.

"I want..." He cleared his throat. "I want to be inside you next time." His timid voice sounded nothing like the Jack who had crudely insisted he was only here for a fuck. Nor did the vulnerable look on his face. This was the real Jack, and he looked nothing like the man who'd waved cash at me, all but calling me a whore.

I climbed off of him and hooked my thumbs into the

waistband of my underpants. Giving him a flirty over-the-shoulder look, I took my time drawing them down my hips, bending to keep them from falling to the floor.

Coming up on his elbow, he whistled. "You're a real-life pinup, you know that?"

I wasn't, but I wiggled my bottom suggestively at him, then turned to present myself to him fully nude. His gaze roamed my body. He looked younger than when he'd stormed past me into the house, more handsome.

"You're really beautiful." His tone was soft, like the look in his eye.

I climbed on top of him and helped him out of his shirt. Lying down on him, I covered his body with mine. I knew he needed this skin-on-skin connection the same way Aaron had needed it.

Aaron spoke often of having only been touched by doctors and nurses in only the most practical and professional ways since his accident. Until he and I were together that first time, he said he hadn't realized how much he'd missed that basic human connection and had been overwhelmed with the realization that he'd stopped thinking of himself as a human being. All he'd been was a patient, not a man.

So I gave the same to Jack, stroking and kissing as much of his bare skin as I could reach. I spent a long time just touching him and connecting with him. Tears leaked out of his eye in a never-ending river. His mouth never stopped moving, murmuring praise and at other times incoherent nonsense. He gave me unfettered access to his body. I kissed his scars and stroked his skin. Besides the patch over his eye and his missing leg, his arm had been amputated just above the elbow and he had a long, thin gash that ran from his rib cage to the opposite hip.

Where Aaron was dark and swarthy, Jack was blond and bright, as though he'd been sprinkled with glitter dust. The room wasn't overly warm, but a fine sheen of sweat made his body glisten, giving off an earthy masculine scent that pooled moisture between my legs. He was an active participant in our lovemaking. It amazed me what he could do to me with only one hand and the little experience I'd rightly guessed he possessed.

I grew needy and desperate from wanting him. When I finally rose over him and sank down onto his member, he let out a deep, strangled sigh that said *finally.*

Yes, finally.

He filled me completely. I rode him, rocking my hips to grind against him. My breasts bounced as I drove up and down on him. The scent of our sex filled the room. He thrust his hips up to meet mine. His breathing grew ragged and I knew he was close so I stroked myself between my legs. Throwing his head back, he drove deep into me and cried out, his fingers digging into my hip.

My climax hit with the force of a bomb. A long low moan ripped through me. I collapsed beside him. Our breath mingled as we gazed at each other. There was so much emotion in his expression that I had to swallow to hold back the feelings he might mistake for pity. I didn't feel at all sorry for this man, this brave, strong warrior. Only joy and a new tender connection that I hoped we could build on. He was good inside, despite all the bad that had happened to him.

I smoothed his sweet lock of hair back and smiled at him. For the first time I got to see a glimpse of what he might have been like before the war.

"I think I love you," he whispered, tears making his eye shine.

"I think I might love you too."

"Marry me?"

I giggled and gave him a hard kiss. "If only I'd met you before my Johnny. I might've taken you up on your offer."

His brows drew together. "You're *married*?"

"No, no, not anymore." I told him all about my Johnny and how I loved him so much I would never marry again.

Sadness crept over Jack's face for a moment and then he gave a brief shake of his head, dislodging it. In its place was a wicked smile.

"I can have you whenever I want then? This doesn't ever have to end?"

"It's up to you when our arrangement ends. You can come to me as often as you'd like."

"As often as I can afford, you mean." I couldn't read his expression.

"It's all I have to give," I said sadly.

"Then it will have to be enough."

He pushed off the bed with his remaining arm and leg, rolling us so that he was on top. His member still inside me, he thrust deep. It took him some time to get the movements down and coordinate his two remaining limbs to do what he used to do with four. Soon he was dripping with sweat and close to climax. I clung to him, my own desire a living, breathing, demanding beast. Rolling his hips, he hit my pleasure spot with every lunge. He focused on my face, his gaze cataloging my expressions as though they were math problems he had to memorize and recite back.

He was still weak in his recovery, but he championed on, giving me a glimpse of the old him before his injuries. He struggled to keep up the pace and I knew he was waiting for me to take my pleasure before he'd take his own. That knowledge sent me tumbling over the edge. His seed poured into me soon after and he collapsed midway, unable to keep himself over me a second longer.

I smoothed his hair back, my heart twisting at the sight of his lips turned up in a small smile. His eye was closed, his face relaxed, which gave me even more pleasure than the physical act we'd shared.

He drifted off to sleep almost immediately. I slipped out from under him and covered him with the bed sheet. In the mid-morning sun he looked so sweet and peaceful I didn't dare disturb him. He slept until it was nearly nightfall. I fed him and then took him to bed again.

When I woke in the morning, he was gone. On my nightstand was more money than we'd agreed to and a note that said he'd come 'round the same time next week.

Jack would prove to be a most faithful and ardent student.

LESSON 3

I was able to put away a good portion of the money Aaron and Jack gave me toward the property taxes, but at the rate we were going, I would still be short when the bill came due. To make matters worse, I lost my part-time job at Feldon's department store to a soldier who had been sent stateside because of a bad heart. He had a family to support. I didn't.

My supervisor offered to give me a recommendation, which wouldn't do me much good. Jobs were scarce for someone like me with no discernable skills. I'd been raised to be a wife, not a secretary. The best I could do was a factory job, but that would mean giving up teaching piano to the children who regularly came to me. One of whom was very talented and dedicated. I couldn't let them down. My *other* lessons with Aaron and Jack could be adjusted, but the children's could not.

I tried to hide as many of my troubles from Aaron as I could. He was too clever by half though and sussed out my worry on one of our afternoons.

He lifted his head from my breast and speared me with his dark eyes. "What's wrong?"

"Nothing. I'm just a little tired I suppose."

"You're a bad liar."

"I lost my job at the store."

"Son of a bitch. Why didn't you tell me?"

"I *am* telling you."

"I mean before..." He motioned to where he was seated deep inside me, large and throbbing.

"Sorry."

"How much do you need?"

I shook my head. This wasn't the time to be having this conversation.

He yanked my hands above my head and held them, then pulled his hips back and slammed back in hard, eliciting an unbidden moan from me. "How." He did it again. "Much?" And again.

He knew I loved it when he got rough with me. "Over nine hundred dollars," I panted.

"How did it get to be that much?"

"The taxes haven't been paid in over five years. I just got a letter."

"Let the house go. Come live with me."

"I can't." This house was all I had left of my Johnny. Aaron knew that.

"He's not in this house, Ruby." He placed a big hand on my chest over my heart. "He's here."

"I know that." I bit my lip and looked away. "But this is where I feel closest to him."

"*I'm* here. *I'm* inside you." To prove his point, he thrust hard into me. "And I'm jealous of a goddamned ghost."

A tear leaked out. "I can't be what you want. I love him and I don't know how to stop."

"Shut up and stop that crying." He crushed his mouth to mine and drove into me over and over at a relentless, brutal pace.

I thrashed beneath his big body. His mouth moved down my neck to my breast and I came apart under him, screaming my Johnny's name.

He didn't stop. He kept pounding into me as though he could force my Johnny out and himself in. I got no rest. He came at me with the force of a tidal wave, bashing against the rocks. I cried out again. Only with my Johnny had I climaxed more than once. Only he could make me wild and uninhibited.

Aaron kept on, pushing me further and further until I was sobbing and climaxing all at the same time.

He let go with a deep guttural growl. He'd always been tender with me, even when he was rough, but not this time. This time was all about him putting his stamp on me. Except it didn't stick. My Johnny was like a physical presence in the bed with us. I could almost see him, smiling and cheering me on and telling me to wring as much as I could out of life because it was short. Too short. For him and for us.

"Honey, listen to me," Aaron gasped, turning my face to his. "I'll get you the money. I'll get you whatever you want. I'll talk to Jack. We'll put our heads together. No more crying, eh?"

I nodded.

He stroked my cheek with his thumb. "We'll get you whatever you want. Whatever you need."

They got me more than that. They got me Henry.

LESSON 4

I was summoned by telegram to appear at an office building in downtown Los Angeles three days later. I had little time to prepare. The telegram gave away nothing, only the barest details—the time, day, address, and the directive that I was to be freshly bathed and wear no undergarments. I was to tell no one where I was going. For this, I would be paid one hundred dollars for half an hour of my time.

The telegram wasn't signed. I didn't dare call Aaron or Jack to ask them what I was in for. They'd been more than generous to me.

Aaron wasn't a rich man, I knew, but he lavished me the best he could. Jack talked me into adding an extra day to his schedule, which I agreed to with the caveat that as soon as the tax bill was paid, we'd go back to our normal routine. Of the two of them, Jack was the most attached and I didn't want to hurt him any more than he'd already been.

I pulled up to an imposing office building on Wilshire Boulevard. It reminded me of the building my father owned and ran his empire out of. I didn't know what kind of business was done in this building, but it must have been very good. An immaculately dressed valet came around my car and opened my door. I was used to being treated this way, from my upbringing, but it had been a long while. I'd forgotten how convenient it could be.

I thanked the valet and headed into the building. A doorman held the door open and wished me a good day. I paused at the reception desk and gave the well-dressed woman behind it the code word I was given in the telegram —tangerine. She made a call and then told me to wait, that someone would come down to get me.

I took a seat in a plush chair and surveyed my surroundings. The outside of the building was a pale imitation of opulence compared to the inside. No expense had been spared. Daddy's building came close to the splendor, but this building outshone it by miles.

After a few moments, a man appeared in front of me. I'd been so busy looking at everything that I hadn't seen him until he spoke and drew my attention.

"Miss Ruby?"

"Yes."

"This way please."

I was led through a hidden side door and down a long hall to an elevator. Compared to the lobby, the hallway was utilitarian and basic to the point of being institutional. Was I being led through the back way?

The elevator was plain too. The man pressed a button for the top floor and we rode up in silence. A thousand questions danced on the tip of my tongue, but I held them back. I got one word of warning from Jack when he told me about the telegram I was to receive—do not ask questions. I knew neither he nor Aaron would lead me anywhere that was unsafe so I was content to follow the man down another hall and through a door marked with an H.

An office. But not just any office. If I thought the reception area was magnificent, this room was a palace. Two of the walls were nearly all glass, giving a splendid view of downtown Los Angeles. Chrome and glass furniture gleamed, but didn't feel cold. Our footsteps were hushed by the plush carpeting that felt as if I were walking on one big pillow.

On the periphery and yet at the center of it all, a smartly dressed man in a suit exquisitely cut to fit his frame stood gazing at the view below, his back to us. Not for the first time since I'd arrived did I wonder why a man who could afford all of this would want or need services from someone like me.

"Sir," my companion said. "Miss Ruby." With that pronouncement, he left through another door that must have led to other offices.

"Have a seat, Miss Ruby," the gentleman at the window said, his voice low yet unusually soft for a man.

I did as I was told, perching at the edge of a chair across the wide expanse of his desk with my hands clasped demurely in my lap.

"You're the piano teacher?" he asked.

"Yes."

"I'm told you handle special cases." He gave the word *special* extra emphasis.

"I consider everyone to be *special* in his or her own way."

"Do you?" He turned then and I couldn't hide my reaction to him.

Pale blond hair framed a face that looked as though it had been fashioned by Gods on a particularly cheerful day in heaven. The pale blue of his eyes matched the sun-bleached sky behind him. He was tall and lean and even standing still he appeared graceful in an effortless way.

It took me a moment to find my voice. "Yes."

"You find me attractive?"

"Yes."

"Hmm, most people do. Of course, I find that my money improves my looks greatly."

"You're handsome regardless of your finances."

"And you're wondering why I would seek out your services."

"Well...yes. I suppose I am."

"I have very—shall we say—*unusual* needs that are rarely met." He drew a case from his inside jacket pocket, selected a cigarette, and lit it. His face, with its beautifully sculpted features, became wreathed in smoke. "I understand you can satisfy them."

"Perhaps if I knew a little bit about what your needs are, I could better answer."

"Take off your dress."

"Excuse me?"

"This won't work if you can't take direction. I'm paying handsomely for your time today, Miss Ruby. Do I need to repeat myself?"

"No." I stood. "Can I at least know your name?"

"Henry."

Lifting my chin in a small act of defiance, I unbuttoned my dress. It was the same one that I'd worn that first time with Jack, with the buttons all the way down the front. As I'd been instructed to wear nothing underneath there was no way to hide my nudity.

Henry did nothing as a revealed myself to him. He stood still, watching and puffing on his cigarette as though he was bored. The full walls of windows bathed me in unforgiving sunlight. If this was the audition, I wasn't likely to get the part. I didn't have perfect skin or the perfect shape. My breasts, while pert, were small compared to my hips and thighs. I looked nothing like the starlets on the movie screens.

I'd never felt more inadequate.

My dress pooled at my feet, leaving me bare as the day I was born. It took everything in me not to fidget under his stare, which roamed my body as though he owned it. And for this half hour, he did. That's what I'd agreed to.

He made a circling motion with his hand. "Turn."

I did as I was told, spinning slowly so that he could see me from all sides.

He pointed behind me. "Lie down on the chaise."

I reclined on the lavish velvet and attempted to look seductive in my pose.

He stubbed out his cigarette and came around the desk. "Spread your legs. I want to see what I'm getting."

I didn't care for his words or his tone, but I opened my legs anyway, keeping my gaze steady and unaffected on his. *One hundred dollars* was a chant in my head. I needed the money. Desperately.

"Wider," he demanded.

I complied, resting my arms across the back of the chaise, opening myself to him as much as possible. Spread eagle and nude, I waited for what he'd do next.

He knelt next to me and leaned forward. Inhaling deeply, he sniffed me from my mouth and neck to my toes, taking longer in some places than others. My sex was of particular interest to him. He spent several minutes smelling me there. He paused to visually examine my folds, then he resumed his scenting of me, finally moving on after several minutes.

When he finished, he sat back on his heels and met my gaze. "You have excellent hygiene."

"Thank you?"

"Have you even been with a woman? Sexually."

"No."

"Would it repulse you?"

"I don't know." I'd heard of men's proclivities for watching women have sexual relations. Is that what he wanted of me? Did he want to participate or just observe? I wasn't sure how I felt about that. Not repulsed as he'd suggested, but not particularly interested either. Curious. I supposed that was the best way to describe my feeling about the suggestion. "I am rather curious though. The mechanics in particular perplex me."

He gave me a smile, the first one I'd gotten from him. "You're honest. I appreciate that. We'll get along well as long as you're honest with me at all times."

I wasn't sure how to respond, so I didn't.

He gestured with an elegant hand toward my sex. "May I?"

I nodded, unsure of just what I was agreeing to. He'd been controlled if aloof with me, so I had a difficult time sorting him out.

He bent his head and put his hot mouth on me. I jolted at the contact, but he held me in place with his large hands on my thighs.

My Johnny had been forward with me like this. I'd grown to love having his mouth and his tongue bringing me to climax. Closing my eyes, I relaxed under Henry and let me legs fall farther apart. If I'd thought my Johnny had been clever about it, Henry was aces. I moaned and writhed on the chaise as he used his lips, tongue, and fingers on me. In short order I was crying out with a hand on his head, holding him down, crudely grinding his mouth against me like a wanton.

I was so caught up in my pleasure that it must've taken him several tries to rouse me because he finally had to grip my wrist and pull my hand away. Stands of his hair were trapped between my fingers and I flushed hot from head to toe.

"I like the way you respond. I think we'll get along *very* well, Miss Ruby." He smiled, his face shiny from my juices. He took a handkerchief from his pocket, shook it out, and wiped his face then his fingers. Eyes closed, he sniffed it, then shoved it back into his pocket.

He rose, smoothed his hair down, adjusted his jacket, and walked to his desk. "You may go now." He lit another cigarette. "There's an envelope on the table near the door you came through with money and further instructions. I trust you to be discrete."

I nodded.

"We have a deal then?"

"Yes." My voice came out wispy, with a lost sound to it that perfectly fit my reaction to this whole interaction.

"Excellent." With that, he turned and resumed his post at the window, ignoring me.

It took me a few moments to get my wobbly legs under me. I messed up the buttons on my dress, making it take twice as long as usual to do them up. By the time I grabbed my pocketbook and headed for the door, I was a little steadier. On the table by the door was an envelope just as he'd said, with a red rose lying on top. I scooped them both up and departed, leaving Henry behind bathed in rings of smoke. In the elevator, I collapsed against the wall and opened the envelope. Inside were the promised hundred dollars and a note. I tucked the envelope into my pocketbook.

A strange liaison, to be sure. The whole business was odd. Yet as I brought the flower to my nose to smell, I had the strangest feeling that Henry, this very, *very* peculiar man with his beautiful features and artful mouth, would alter my life in much the same way as my Johnny had.

LESSON 5

The instructions on the note in the envelope Henry had given me indicated that I should show up exactly one week after our first meeting to the address listed at nine o'clock PM sharp. I was to be freshly bathed, not have had any relations that day, and to wear nothing under my clothes, the same as I had when I'd first met him.

I'd had to rearrange my days with Jack to accommodate Henry, as I was to have seen him that day. The note was very clear about that being against the rules. Jack was a bit put out, as it meant that I would see him one less day this week, but he managed to be stoic about it.

To soothe him, I promised to try a technique with him that I'd read about in a book that was rather blue. I'd gotten the book at a used bookstore. It was very enlightening on the subject of relations and quite direct, in that it was the first time I'd ever seen photographs of couples engaging in sexual acts. It shocked and titillated me in its suggestion that both women and men could benefit from the insertion of fingers or a phallus in the anus. I'd heard of such acts of course, but had never practiced them.

Jack was most enthusiastic to try. When I'd hung up the telephone after our call, I realized his excitement might stem from a misunderstanding. He may or may not have been operating under the impression that I would allow him to put his member in my anus. I'd stood with my hand still on the telephone, contemplating that thought for several minutes. In the end, I'd discovered that I wasn't against the notion, and turned to the book for guidance on how Jack and I might best go about the process the next time we met.

As directed, I took a taxi to the address Henry had given me, to a private home high in the Hollywood Hills. The fare was quite exorbitant from Long Beach to Hollywood and I nearly fainted at the price the cabbie quoted me.

When I arrived at the house, a man in a uniform came out to greet me and paid the cab fare in cash, adding in a handsome tip. The taxi drove away and I was left alone with the uniformed man. A shiver swept through me, partly from the cool night air blowing up my skirt, chilling my naked extremities, and partly from the eerie sense of the unknown.

Again I reminded myself that Henry had not behaved badly toward me. Quite the opposite. I pressed my thighs together in remembrance of how quickly and thoroughly he'd brought me to pleasure. Additionally, Jack would not recommend me to someone who would do me harm. This I was sure of, as he was intensely devoted to me and at the very least he'd want me to survive in order for us to try anal sex the next time he came to me.

Henry's uniformed man led me up the steps of the house, which was sprawling in size and grandiose in appearance. Again I wondered why a man like Henry, with such a vast fortune, would want to hire someone like me to have relations with. Surely women were falling all over him.

Remembering his comment about his *specific needs*, I couldn't help but wonder how base and unusual those needs could be that he couldn't find women to satisfy them. Not even women he paid. Jack had told me precious little about Henry, other than they'd met through his father's business and had become friendly enough to discuss me and my special relationship with Jack. Although how the subject came up, I'll probably never know. Men, despite my varied experiences, were a mystery to me.

I followed Henry's man through a magnificent foyer, up a grand staircase, down a wide hall past what felt like dozens of doors to a set of double doors at the end of the hall.

The man stopped and gestured for me to let myself in. "Mr. Henry will be with you shortly." He bowed briefly, then walked back the way we'd come, leaving me alone.

"Into the Land of Oz," I whispered to myself and opened the door.

The room was completely white. Everywhere. It was like walking into a snowdrift. I was temporarily struck dumb by the starkness. Yet it wasn't cold. On the contrary, it held a warmth that drew me in.

Turning a circle, I tried to take in as much of the room as I could before Henry arrived and caught me gawking. Two fireplaces warmed the soft space that felt like a down comforter, wrapped around me. A large bed held prominence in the room, piled high with snowy pillows and draped in gauzy fabric. Lounge chairs and chaises filled the remainder of the space except for one corner, where a blindingly white grand piano stood.

I was drawn to it as if I was made of metal and it was a magnet. I'd never seen a piano so exquisitely detailed and shiny. It spoke to me, to my soul, where my music lived. I'd managed to plunk along nicely on the old upright that had been my Johnny's mother's since marrying him and leaving home. I hadn't realized how much I'd missed having access to an instrument such as this to play.

I sat down hesitantly at its keys. Feeling a bit like a child who could be caught at any moment, I placed my fingers on the keys and closed my eyes. The first chords of Debussy's "Clair de Lune" floated into the air. I hadn't meant to play, only to touch the beautiful instrument, but it was as though my fingers had thoughts of their own and before I knew it, my whole being was in the piece.

I leaned into the notes, swaying as though buffeted by strong winds. The music carried me to other lands, through other times. I became other people doing other things. I was outside the room, outside my body. The notes flowed through me, weaving in and out. I could smell them and taste them and feel them in every cell of my body. I was the music and yet not. It existed without me, using me. I was merely it's pawn, and the music my master.

As the last notes slowly faded, I became aware that I wasn't alone. Opening my eyes, I started at the sight of Henry leaning against the piano. He was bare-chested, wearing only loose pajama pants the same white as the rest of the room. He was marvelously made, his muscles sculpted and toned. Twin scars that ran horizontally on either side of his torso across his rib cage were the only imperfections, which for me was no imperfection whatsoever.

My heart tripped a fluttery beat in my chest at the look in his eyes.

"You play beautifully," he said, his voice thick and heavy. "Take off your dress and play something else for me."

My faced flushed hot. For some reason his directness

brought out the shy schoolgirl in me. He made me feel wanton and terribly, terribly naughty. I was no virgin yet everything felt new with him.

I slid out from behind the piano and undid my dress, letting it pool to the floor at my feet. His gaze scorched me head to toe. I forced myself to resist the urge to cover myself under his stare. It was that moving and provocative. My breasts grew heavy and tight. A thin trickle of wetness dampened the curls between my legs. His look was a touch, stroking me and making me want to both shield myself from his attention and display myself for his approval. Never had I felt such contradictory emotions at one time.

"When we're together, you are to never be dressed," he demanded. "Understood?"

I inclined my head.

"Sit." He gestured toward the piano.

The bench was cool beneath my bare bottom, a stark contrast between the heat flowing through me and the warmth of the room. He came up behind me and straddled me, pulling me up so that I rested partially on the bench and partially between his thighs. His skin was hot against mine. He cupped my breasts in his large hands. More heat infused my already overwhelmed senses.

"Play," he commanded.

"W-what should I play?"

"Anything you like." One of his hands drifted lower, sliding between my parted legs.

I stumbled through the notes of Tchaikovsky's "Piano Concerto No. 1" as though I was only learning it and hadn't played it a thousand times before. He kept me on the edge with his hands on my body and his mouth on my neck. Every time I'd lose my place or try to stop playing, he'd tweak my nipple and tell me to finish it or he wouldn't let *me* finish. It was a torturous mission. He didn't play fair.

It was as though we'd been together a thousand times. He knew my body that well. I'd get to the crest of pleasure and he'd bring me back down again slowly, then rebuild it until I was panting and fumbling the keys again. He did this over and over.

"Henry, please," I begged as the final chords of the song rang in the air. "*Please*."

He lifted me up, pushing me down across the piano, making the keys clang discordantly. My breasts pressed against the cold edge of the piano and the keys bit into my thighs. The bench clattered somewhere behind us as he pressed me harder into the wood. His fingers probed me from behind and then I felt his member pushing at my entrance. I was so slick from his fingering that he slid into me beautifully right to the hilt.

Gripping my hips, he pounded into me. Never had I been taken so roughly or so thoroughly.

He came at me with everything he had. Before too long I gasped, nearing my climax. When my pleasure hit it was as though I'd been thrown into another realm. Crying out his name, my legs went weak. Were it not for him behind me, holding me up, I'd have dissolved into a puddle at his feet. He held me there, pushed up against the piano as he shuddered out his own release.

With a hand on the back of my head, keeping me pinned where I was, he pulled out of me. The loss of him made me whimper. I could've stayed like that with him inside me forever.

"Don't move," he ordered.

I did as he asked. My breath came in hot pants as I struggled to regain myself. Never again would I look at the hammers and strings inside a piano without thinking of Henry and the naughty things he'd just done to me. Nor would I ever play Tchaikovsky's piano concerto without remembering the way Henry's hands had felt on my bare flesh.

"You are a wonder," he whispered in my ear as he brought me back against him, filling his hands with my breasts. "I must taste you."

My head spun as he lowered the top of the piano and replaced the cover over the keys. Then he lifted me and laid me on top, my feet resting on the keyboard cover. I was so overwrought, all I could do was let him stage me the way he wanted.

He set the bench upright and sat upon it between my spread thighs. His mouth was hot and hungry on my exposed sex. He began with gentle licks, tiny flicks of sensation. Pressing my legs open wider, he increased his ministrations. In no time I writhed atop the piano, moaning and carrying on as though I'd die without release.

I was beginning to see that it would always be this way with Henry. It had been the same with my Johnny. I was shameless with him, begging for what I wanted and insisting he should give it to me now. My Johnny had given me everything and then some. Henry was proving to be just as skilled, just as aggressive in his pursuit of my pleasure. There was nothing for me to do but give in to him and his dark demands.

LESSON 6

I awoke the next morning in the big white bed thoroughly used and alone. Sitting up, I looked around for some sign that Henry was close. The silken sheet slid down my body, revealing the marks he'd put on me. Love bites, my Johnny would've called them. Henry had marked me. I'd never allowed Jack or Aaron such liberties. It had been my experience that men, while they didn't mind a woman's boldness in bed, never liked to be reminded that they weren't the only one she gave her affection to.

My cheeks heated at the thought of explaining to my other two gentlemen callers just why I'd allowed a third man to do to me what I'd patently refused them. What did that say about the change Henry had brought over me? Was it me somehow subconsciously allowing myself to be owned by Henry in ways that I'd only ever allowed my Johnny? Did this mean that I no longer wanted to entertain the affections of Aaron and Jack? For surely they'd take one look at me, in my present condition, and refuse to lie with me. The ego of man was a fragile, fragile thing.

I rose from the bed and stretched. Every part of me was

sore, especially between my legs. Henry had used me in more ways and more times in one night than I was accustomed to. A delicious thrill raced through me at the remembrance of all the pleasure he'd given me. He had more stamina and comeback than any man I'd even been with, including my Johnny.

The thoughts drifted in like unwelcome ghosts, casting their doubt. Thoughts I'd firmly set aside every time Henry had entered me. He wasn't here now to chase them away so they lingered and grew roots.

I slid a hand between my legs. Dry. As many times as Henry had taken his pleasure inside of me, I should be full of him upon rising. So full that it should trickle down my legs. But there was nothing. And then I thought of all the times he'd pushed my hands away when I'd tried to touch him, or turned me around so I'd faced away, and how he'd never been nude with me, having worn his pajama bottoms all night.

I ran a hand over the sheets. It was the same. We should've soaked the sheets with our combined fluids. My confusion grew until it filled my head, washing shame over me in hot waves. Henry had been good to me. I should be grateful. He paid me handsomely and treated me with care. He gave me unmeasured pleasure with his hands and his mouth and his...

My thoughts stalled. Henry was generously endowed. He'd filled me multiple times. His powerful thrusts brought me to pleasure over and over again. But there was something not quite right about the whole business.

If I'd had no experience I might not have noticed. I could never feign virginity or innocence. I was a fallen woman. A woman men paid to lie with. I knew what I was and the names people used—tart, wanton...whore. I was all of those things and more and yet I wasn't ashamed. I gave as much as I got. It was an equitable exchange of pleasure. My gentlemen always came back for more. Henry was no exception. Except that he was. What was the protocol in such circumstances?

The bedroom door opened and Henry strode in carrying a tray laden with food. He took in my appearance, his gaze silkily stroking my skin like a touch. He wore a robe over his bare chest and pajama bottoms. I was struck all over again by his handsomeness. He was beautiful, heartbreakingly so.

"Good morning," he said. "I've brought you sustenance."

The question I'd first posed in his office the day we'd met came flying at me from out of nowhere. "Why am I here? You could have anyone. *Why me*?"

He set the tray down on top of the piano, rattling the dishes. "This again."

"I'm not especially beautiful. I'm not as worldly and sophisticated as I once was. I'm a widow, a whore who sells her body to finance her existence. You could be with debutants and starlets. What are you doing with me?"

"I thought we went over this." He pulled his cigarette case from his robe pocket and lit one, keeping his gaze steady on me. But there was something dark behind his eyes, something that made me lean back in defense.

"You said that your needs are unusual," I pressed. "What *needs*? From the things we've done, your needs aren't any different from those of other men. There are some peculiarities—"

"My needs," he ground out, "are mine to share or not share. Frankly you aren't in a position to question me. I pay for your body, not your thoughts."

I flinched at his words. He'd never spoken to me like this before, but then I'd said the same about myself. I shouldn't be shocked by them. The thoughts about him drifted in again, demanding to be answered. "Is there something the matter with you, some condition you haven't shared—"

"Silence!" He stubbed out his cigarette on the tray. "On your hands and knees. Now."

"Henry—"

"If I wanted your mouth, I'd wrap it around my cock. *On your knees.*"

I started to obey, partly out of fear and partly out of salacious curiosity.

"Turn around," he said. "Then down. On the floor."

I did as I was told, presenting Henry with my bare backside. I couldn't help the shiver that went through me as he knelt behind me and put his hands between my legs.

"You're wet. Does talking back to me excite you?" He wrapped his fist in my hair and pulled back gently to bring my head up. "Is this what you want?" He ground his erection against my backside. "Have I not given it to you enough?"

"You have. I just... Why can't I touch you?" I reached a hand between my legs, grazing his member with my fingertips. "I want to touch you, take you in my mouth and pleasure you."

He reached around me and grasped my wrist, bringing my arm behind my back, but not hurting me. "I'm the one in charge here. I say what happens."

"I'd understand. I've heard of prosthetics—"

He used his size and strength to topple me over onto my back and came down on top of me. His breathing came in harsh, heavy pants. There was something like panic in his expression that made me want to reach out and soothe his brow.

"I thought you were different," he whispered. "I thought..."

"I am. This?" I pointed to his love bite on my breast. "I've only ever allowed my Johnny to mark me, make me his. Only him, and now you." I took his face in my hands. "I just want to be close to you, to understand you. You had to know I would figure it out eventually. I can't be the first."

He laid his head in the crook of my neck. "You're not demanding money for your silence?"

"Is that what others have done?" It all made sense now. Why he paid me instead of dating the kind of women a man like him would want on his arm. "I'm not like them."

"I know. I think I knew that from the first moment I met you. I want to be inside you. I want you to come apart under me, screaming my name. But I need you to not question me anymore on this. I need you to not look at me or try to touch me. I need you to pretend..." His voice broke on the last word. "I'm a real man."

"You *are* a real man."

"No. I'm not. But being with you..." He raised his head and looked down at me. "I feel like one."

"Come inside me." I pushed my pelvis into his, rubbing against his prosthesis. "Make me feel you. Give me pleasure and let me give it to you. I promise not to look or touch." I slipped my thumb into his mouth. "Lie with me, Henry. Make me yours once more."

He pulled back a little, fumbling with the front of his pajama bottoms. His gaze stayed on mine as he pushed into me. I arched up as he filled me, my eyes drifting closed.

"No," he said. "Look at me. See *me*."

"I do see you, Henry. Don't you get it? I've only ever seen you. Not this room, this house, your wealth and status...or your secret. I see only you."

He thrust into me harder, making me gasp. "I want to see you come. I want you looking at me when I push you over. I want you to know it's me who can give you this." He punctuated his point with a grind of his hips that sent me spiraling toward orgasm.

I grasped my breasts in my hands, rolling my nipples. Close. So close.

"That's it, love," he coaxed. "Come for me."

I broke into a thousand pieces under him. He rotated his hips a few more times, rubbing deliciously against me, and then he too found his pleasure, crying out my name. I brought him down and crushed my lips to his. Our mouths met in a mad frenzy, then slowed as the last flickers of ecstasy pulsed through me.

As my heart rate slowed I became aware of several things at once—Henry's body heavy and warm on top of me, the silkiness of his hair between my fingers, and a sudden unexpected realization. My mind scrambled to wrap around the unwelcome thought.

This was his fantasy and it was my job to fulfill it, I reminded myself. Not question it. I'd already pushed too hard and gone too far. I could've lost him. If I didn't control my wayward thoughts and just live in the illusion, I *would* lose him. Of this I was certain. So I smiled up at him as he gazed down at me with a satisfied grin on his face. I could almost read his thoughts as he stroked the hair back from my face.

He was becoming so much more to me than either Aaron or Jack had and possibly ever would. I think I knew the moment I met him that he would change my life in much the same way I knew my Johnny would when I'd first met him. Everything Henry had said and done to me in his office that first day came flooding back to me. And I knew. I *knew*.

Tears leaked out of the corners of my eyes.

"Hey," he said in a bit of a panic, thumbing away the wetness. "What's this? Why are you crying? Did I hurt you?"

I shook my head. "No. I don't think you could ever do that."

"Then what is it?"

"I'm just happy."

"These are happy tears?" He brought his thumb to his mouth. "They don't taste like happy tears."

"They are. I promise."

He lowered himself so our bodies touched again, resting his weight on his forearms. "Why don't I believe you?"

"Believe this: you'll always be safe with me. Your secrets are mine. In the short time I've known you, we've built a connection that goes beyond the physical. I know you feel it too."

He lowered his head in agreement.

"Whatever your needs are, just know that I can meet them. I *want* to meet them."

His gaze flickered up to mine and his lips parted as though he meant to say something, then he pressed them together and gave a brief nod.

"We'll leave things as they are for however long you want. It's up to you. I'm happy to go along as we are and equally as happy to take it further."

"Thank you." His voice was gruff, his eyes shiny. His gaze roamed my face as though he were looking for something in my expression or trying to read my thoughts, then he shook his head and he was back to the Henry who was in control. He pressed his lips to mine and slid out of me. "I've occupied you too much." I kept my gaze on his face as he adjusted his pajama bottoms. "You must be sore. Come." He rose and held his hand out to me. "Let's breakfast and talk of other things."

He held out a silken robe for me to slip into. It felt like heaven against my skin. "I *am* hungry." My stomach chose that moment to heartily agree and I clapped a hand over it in embarrassment.

Laughing, he took my hand and led me to the piano where he'd left our food. "You must maintain your strength. I have lots of plans for you."

LESSON 7

Henry's man drove me home after breakfast. As he held me during our goodbye, I got the impression Henry didn't want me to leave, but he had an empire to run and couldn't stay in bed with me all day.

On the way home I mulled over our time together, coming to a couple of conclusions and a decision. The timing would have to be just right to pull it off. I wasn't entirely sure I could do it though. My doubts about Henry and me had nothing to do with me and everything to do with him. He was a very proud man. As well he should be.

What little I'd gleaned about him from Jack, the few scant newspaper articles, some library research, and from Henry himself told me that I had a very tall mountain to climb. Most women wouldn't make the effort. They'd take his money, his gifts, the pleasure he offered, and go away happy. Apparently I wasn't like most women. There was a connection between us that I wanted to deepen and the only way to do that would be to lay everything out between us. No secrets. No shame.

He hadn't asked it, but I had the strong feeling Henry

wished he had me all to himself. I owed *so much* to Jack and Aaron, including my meeting Henry.

My Henry.

I sighed and glanced out the car window. I couldn't break things off with the other two gentlemen. I wouldn't. If Henry had verbalized his wishes I wouldn't comply, even if it meant Henry would end things between us. My loyalty and dignity meant everything to me. Jack and Aaron had been good to me. They cared for me. I was bound by honor to respect them and honor our agreements for as long as they wished.

The car rounded the corner of my little street. Aaron's truck was parked at the curb. His dark head was bent as he sat on my stoop so he didn't see me pull up until the driver closed the car door behind me. He took in the vehicle and the driver, then his gaze slid over to me and stuck. I smiled and gave him a small wave. His expression didn't change as he stood and brushed off the seat of his jeans. I realized he was staring at the love bite on my neck. Self-consciously I put a hand over it as I reached him.

"Hi," I said, feeling awkward for the first time with him. "What are you doing here?"

He reached up and pulled my hand down. "Guess I know what kept you." There was an edge to his voice.

"We don't have an appointment for today."

"Actually we do. We rescheduled from last week. I was supposed to get an extra." He glanced at his wristwatch, still holding my arm. "You're nearly half an hour late." He leaned forward, putting his face to my neck, and inhaled. "I can smell him on you."

"I'm sorry. I forgot. Come inside." I rushed past him to the door and opened it.

When I turned around he was watching Henry's car

drive down the street. "He pays you more than I do." He said it contemplatively, as though he were commenting on the weather or a sporting event.

"Come inside." I stood just inside the door, holding it open for him.

He shoved his hands in his pockets and did as I asked. Stopping in front of me, he eyed the mark on my neck. "What other *extras* does his money buy?"

I swung at him without thinking.

He easily caught my wrist in his big hand. We stared at one another, our chests heaving, eyes angry. He'd never spoken to me like this before. I wasn't sure I liked this side of him. He stroked the inside of my wrist with the pad of his thumb.

"What are you doing?" I asked, breathless, unable to rein in my physical response to him.

I was sore from Henry, but still I wanted Aaron. My body reacted to his nearness, my sex becoming wet and my nipples pebbling. As per Henry's instructions, I wore nothing beneath my dress. Aaron noticed, his hot, hungry gaze raking over me. His free hand gathered my skirt, bunching and lifting it up. His fingers grazed the bare flesh of my thighs. No stockings. No underpants. I was vulnerable to his probing fingers. The front door still stood open, but anyone walking by would only see us standing close together.

"Is this how he likes it?" he asked, running a finger through the dampening curls between my thighs. "What else does his money buy?"

"Aaron—" I started.

He ground his erection against my belly. "What else?"

"Some exclusivity."

"Hmm, which is why I get you used. Sloppy seconds."

"It's not like that." I went to put my hand on his cheek to soothe him, but he captured it and clamped it together with my other hand against the wall above my head. "You know it isn't."

"The thing is, I don't." He slid a finger inside me, then another.

I gasped and winced a little, my hips projecting forward of their own accord. His sudden directness, born of jealousy or something else—I didn't know—excited me. I wanted him. Right here in my entryway with the door open. I peeked outside. The street was empty. When I glanced back at him he had a cat-who-got-the-cream smile on his face.

He used the rhythm he knew I liked to draw me toward my pleasure. Lowering his head, he put his hot mouth on my breast over my dress and sucked hard. I bucked and struggled, not really wanting to get away from him.

"Aaron," I weakly protested. "The door."

"Will stay open," he said over my breast, the wet fabric chilling without his mouth on it. "You're mine. At least for the time I'm paying you. And I want the whole world to know. I want them to watch."

Three fingers entered me, pistoning in and out. He still held my hands captive above my head. I writhed against him. A low moan escaped me. He fumbled with the front of his pants, sucking hard at my breast.

"Hurry," I panted.

He freed himself and bent at the knees to get the right angle. His thrust was hard and punishing. He came at me like a man possessed. Sealing his mouth over mine, he caught my screams of desire. Anyone walking or driving by the house could see us. The thought only drove me higher and I broke. Aaron shoved deep and let himself go, clamping his mouth over the love bite on my neck that Henry had given me.

Panic flooded me at Aaron's attempt to erase my time with Henry. I pushed at him. He lifted his head.

"Let me go." I struggled to punctuate my point.

He released my hands, but his big body still pinned me to the wall, his manhood buried deep inside me.

I swung and connected this time. His head jerked to the side. The resounding crack echoed in the confining space.

He slowly turned his head back toward me. His eyes blazed with unmistakable fire. "You were mine first. You will always *be* mine."

I shook my head. "I'm Johnny's. Always was. Always will be."

He rocked his pelvis, reminding me that he still impaled me. He was still hard. "That's not Johnny inside you."

"Get out."

He closed the door, sealing us inside. "You don't get it." He pulled out a little and came at me in gentle, easy strokes. "I *like* having you after he's had you. I like the smell of him on you and his marks on your body. I like knowing my seed is mixing with his. You got out of that car looking like you'd been ravaged all night long and I was instantly and insanely hard for you. I don't expect you to understand it. I surely don't. But I'm dying to see where else he's been, where else he's marked you, so I can put my mouth there too.

"You feel me, Ruby?" He punctuated his point with a long, slow slide that hit deep. "Ain't never been this hard before. I can hardly see for wanting you. Take your dress off. I want to see the rest of you."

His admission shocked and excited me, but I was feeling my night with Henry and Aaron's earlier assault. "You've got to be gentle. I'm sore, Aaron. He had me over and over. I've never had it so many times in one night. Please. Please be gentle with me."

"Aww, babe. It makes me crazy to hear you talk like that." He put his mouth by my ear. "Did he bend you over and take you from behind?" I nodded and he growled low in his throat. "Take your dress off."

He continued his slow, gentle slide in and out of me as I worked the buttons of my dress. It parted in inches. He couldn't take his eyes off my fingers and the skin that was gradually revealed. I put my arms back and let it slide to the floor. I was nude now and he was still fully dressed. He traced a soft finger over the love bites Henry had given me.

"He make you scream his name?"

Getting into it, I nodded. "I lost count of how many times."

A shudder went through him. "I don't know if I can be gentle with you," he rasped. "I don't want to hurt you."

"It's okay. You're doing okay. Take me to bed."

"He did all this," he touched the marks, "in bed?"

"Some of it."

I could tell the physical strain of holding back for me was getting to him. "Where else did he have you?"

"On the piano the first time. On the floor the last time."

Sweat beaded his forehead. "And where else in between?"

"A couch. The bathtub. Against the wall. Bent over the bathroom vanity."

"He had you six times last night?"

"Seven."

His muscles bunched. He was hard all over from holding back. "Jesus," he rasped.

"You want to bend me over the table, Aaron? You want to take me like he did?"

"Yeah. Just like he did." He reluctantly pulled out of me and reached behind him to pull his shirt over his head.

"Leave it. He stayed dressed the whole time. I want you to do that too."

He bobbed his head and swallowed hard, then followed me to the dining room.

"Push me down," I instructed. "He was forceful, demanding. And I did everything he told me to do."

He swiped his arm across his forehead, wiping away the sweat, then he put a hand on my back and pushed me down. My breasts pressed against the cold wood and made my sore nipples harden further.

"Widen your legs."

I immediately complied and earned a grunt of approval. I yelped at the feel of his mouth on my backside in exactly the same spot as Henry had put his mouth. I began to imagine having both men at once. One at the front of me and one at the back, but I knew Henry would never share me like that.

Aaron rose and slid his hand up and down my back as he positioned himself at my entrance. I was so excited that he glided easily inside me. Gripping my hips, he made his thrusts. Gentle at first, just the way I'd asked, then more forceful. He matched his fingers to the marks on my waist where Henry had held me and pounded into me.

"Pull my hair," I gasped.

The hungry sound he made as he wrapped his hand in my hair and pulled back made my sex flood with renewed desire.

He really came at me then, knocking my hips against the table and making me wince. I pushed back into him to relieve the pain. That only seemed to spur him on. I cried out, screaming Henry's name. Aaron came instantly, driving deep into me and releasing his seed a second time. He collapsed over me, his body hot and heavy on mine, but not so I was crushed beneath him. His breath wheezed in and out in harsh pants.

I was very sore then and just wanted him out of me. "Aaron?"

He grunted, as though he were incapable of any other sound.

"Can you release me now?"

He roused himself and moved off and out of me. I straightened gingerly. I'd been used too many times in too many ways.

He watched my careful movements with a grimace of regret. "I was too rough."

"I'll be okay. Nothing a soak in the bath won't cure."

His gaze dropped to the V of my legs. He reached out and swiped a finger through his seed dripping out of me. "He fill you that much? So much that it ran down your legs?"

I nodded, lying. "In rivers. The sheets were soaked."

He palmed his member, which was rallying back at astonishing speed, his gaze hot and hungry once more. "Get on the table."

I obeyed.

"Open your legs. I want to see it flow out of you."

I did as he asked, propping each foot on a chair.

"Tell me what he did to you and how he did it. I want to hear *all* of it."

"He insists I wear no undergarments."

He inclined his head, no doubt remembering the state I was in when I arrived.

"I'm to be unclothed at all times, while he keeps his clothes on. He's hard all the time. Like you are now. He fed me, worshipped me. Gave me so much pleasure I lost track of time. He insists I be clean. I can't have been with another man before him. He smells me. That was one of the things he said he liked best about me, how I smell...down there." I pointed to my sex, which was steeped in Aaron's seed. It poured out of me into a puddle on the table and beaded in the curls between my legs.

Aaron grabbed a chair, pulled it close, and sat between my parted thighs. His gaze solely focused on my center. He stroked himself in earnest as he leaned forward and inhaled. I smelled of sex, my own juices, Henry, and Aaron. The scent aroused me. If I could tolerate him once more I'd invite him inside me. But I was really starting to feel the soreness now despite my arousal. Maybe there was a way to satisfy us both.

"He put his mouth on me there," I told Aaron. "Several times. He made me cry out over and over. He could spend hours between my thighs, he told me."

"You like a man's mouth on you here?" He traced a light finger across my folds.

"Very much. Henry is particularly talented in that way. Reminds me of my Johnny."

"He taste himself *and* you?"

"Many times." Another lie. I hated keeping the truth from Aaron, but I owed it to Henry to keep his secret. If the roles were reversed I'd do the same for Aaron. It was my duty.

Aaron lowered his head and breathed me in. He put his hands on my thighs, widening them farther. He seemed obsessed with recreating everything Henry had done to me. The first swipe of his tongue was tentative. He glanced up at me. I nodded in encouragement and leaned back, giving him more access.

I parted my folds and pointed to the little swollen nub at the top. "Stroke me lightly here. Keep the same rhythm, steady and constant."

He did as instructed and soon I was panting. I lay back across the table and took my breasts in my hands, rolling my nipples and increasing the sensations. All the while Aaron stroked himself, changing hands, using my juices to lubricate his organ. It was carnal, sinful, and erotic. Aaron's inexperience was eclipsed by his tenacity and willingness to follow direction *exactly*. Soon I writhed on the table, my sighs and mewls mixing with the sucking sound of his hand on his member, his approving moans, and his tongue lapping.

I tensed and grabbed the back of Aaron's head as I cried out for Henry. His grunt morphed into a groan and I lifted my head to see his seed pouring over his hand as he pumped out the final spurts. His last act before moving away was to clamp his mouth on the inside of my thigh exactly where Henry had marked me.

I flopped back on the table, completely spent. I needed a bath and a nap, in that order. Two different men had used me in just about every way possible in the past twenty-four hours.

I should've felt degraded or ashamed. Instead I felt empowered. I'd brought my lovers to their knees to satisfy me. These big, masterful men had practically bent themselves inside out to bring me to pleasure multiple times. There was power in that and I held it.

Aaron laid his head on my stomach to catch his breath and, I realized, to be close to me. I sifted my fingers through his hair, enjoying the moment. Soon he would be gone and I would be alone again. Without him here, none of it would feel real. Almost as though I'd imagined it all—last night with Henry and Aaron's reaction to seeing me come home thoroughly ravaged, and everything that had come after. With him here, solid and worshiping, it all was real. And it had happened...to *me*. I smiled to myself.

Aaron reluctantly roused himself and raised his head. "What are you smiling at?"

I ran my fingers through the hair at his temple. "You."

"I did good?"

"You couldn't tell?"

"Yeah." A blush crept up his neck. "I guess I could." He looked at me for a long moment. Expressions flickered across his face so quickly that I couldn't catalog them all.

"What is it?"

"I intended this to be our last appointment."

"Oh." I sat up. "Why?"

"I met someone. A woman." His gaze shifted away. "We've gone out a few times. I like her. A lot."

I stuffed down my disappointment. I would miss him. Terribly. I smiled and stroked the side of his face. "That's wonderful, Aaron. I'm so happy for you."

"Do you think...?" He cleared his throat and looked up at me. "You could see me still? After you've been with him? Not every time, but... You, seeing you...like this..." He gestured toward my well-used body. "I like it. And well, I don't think...she's not the kind of woman to... She comes from a good family...works as a teacher... She has a reputation..."

"And you don't think she'd want to do the kinds of things you and I do together?"

He shook his head. "She's a virgin."

"Well, you know, I was a virgin once too, when I met my Johnny. He was gentle and encouraging with me. He taught me a lot, made me feel comfortable and confident. If you could do that for your lady, I don't see any reason why she wouldn't open up for you."

"You really think so?"

"I know so. If she loves you and you love her, I don't see any reason why the two of you can't have a fulfilling relationship like I did with my Johnny."

"It probably wouldn't be proper then for me to still come to you."

"Not if you care for her and you want a life with her. Still coming to see me...well, it might hurt her. You don't want that, do you?"

"No."

"Do you want to marry her?"

He considered my question. "Yes. I think I do."

"Then maybe this should be goodbye for you and me."

He laid his head in my lap and wrapped his arms around my waist. "I don't want to give you up."

"I know." I caressed his head. "I don't want to give you up either. You were my first after my Johnny. You're special to me. I'll never forget you."

"I'll never forget you. Or today. Or any of it."

We parted with a soft kiss. He didn't look back as he went down the walk and I didn't stand in the doorway to watch him go.

LESSON 8

I spent every weekend and two nights a week with Henry. Every moment with him felt like a gift. He saw to my every need, be it carnal, physical or emotional. He lavished me with presents and more pleasure than I could almost bear.

In return, I played for him. Sitting at his beautiful grand piano, my fingers coaxing music from the keys, was the greatest gift of all. I played modern tunes at his request and the melancholy songs I preferred in my youth. The sadness of the notes always prompted Henry to find new and inventive ways to chase away any lingering blues.

It got to where I hardly had any time anymore for Jack. He noticed, and protested every chance he got. I felt bad for cutting down his days, but with Henry's rule there was no help for it. He wasn't like Aaron. He didn't like sharing. Which meant that I had to plan my schedule so that there would be at least twelve hours between the time I was with Jack and the time I was with Henry. Once, I'd seen Jack the afternoon before my night with Henry, and although I'd bathed thoroughly, trying to erase my time with Jack, Henry caught on.

I'd never seen him so furious. Angry for Henry wasn't like it was for other men. He grew quiet, deadly calm. His silence scared me more than if he'd shouted and railed. Even more than if he'd punched something the way my father had done when he'd had one of his fits. The walls of my father's office had taken quite a beating over the years. It seemed there were always men in there patching holes. Which would also set him off. Living with that kind of anger, I learned to get out of the way quickly.

There was nowhere to go with Henry. We were in his bedroom surrounded by all of that white and he was giving me a most passionate hello kiss when he went eerily still. At first I thought he might have been joking when he'd sniffed me and stood up straighter than a soldier in the middle of unbuttoning my dress, glaring at me with narrowed eyes.

"You broke my rule." His voice set off warning sirens inside me. "I can *smell* him."

I opened my mouth to refute it, but he interrupted me.

"Don't deny it. Don't pile lies upon your betrayal. I'm paying for more than your body. I expect your honesty and to follow my simple rules."

I clamped my mouth shut. He turned on his heel and left the room. I stood there for several minutes, trying to figure out what to do.

The door opened again and his butler came into the room. "Mr. Henry has instructed me to bathe you."

"*Excuse* me?"

He spoke in slow, measured words as if I were simple. "I've been instructed to bathe you."

I clutched the front of my dress together. "No."

"Mr. Henry was very clear." He said it as though Henry asked him to bathe his guests every day.

"I don't care how clear he was. I won't allow it."

"Very well." He left the room without another word.

I worked the buttons of my dress, doing them back up as quickly as possible. I didn't know if Henry would come back or the butler.

Standing in the middle of the snowstorm room, I had a moment where I suddenly realized where I was and what I was doing. If my parents could see me now, the whore of a rich man, they'd disown me in a flash if they hadn't already done so. There wouldn't be enough walls in the world for my father to bash. I thought of my Johnny and the sad look he'd have on his face as he shook his head and reminded me that I was precious, far more special than I'd ever given myself credit for. He'd always thought better of me than I thought of myself. How far I've fallen from my days with him.

Tears filled my eyes thinking of my one true love, my Johnny. Why did he have to leave me? If he hadn't, I wouldn't be where I was, falling for a man who paid for and controlled my body. In that moment I both hated and loved the two men who'd captured my heart. I should've just walked out of this palace and never looked back. I could get by with the money Jack gave me. He didn't fill the same space in my heart as Henry did, but maybe that was for the best.

The door opened again and the butler appeared once more. "Mr. Henry will see you another time. The car is waiting out front to take you home."

I was being *dismissed*? "Where is *Mr.* Henry?"

"In the library."

I strode past him into the hall. "Where is the library?" I asked without stopping.

The butler trotted along after me. "Miss Ruby. The car."

"I'm not leaving until I see Henry." I hit the bottom of the stairs and started for the first door I saw.

"That's the parlor. Really, miss, *the car*."

I headed for the next door.

"The dining room. You can't just wander around—"

"I wouldn't have to if you'd tell me which is the library."

"Mr. Henry doesn't like being interrupted—"

"Well, Miss Ruby doesn't like being assigned a bath by a stranger, then told to leave without so much as a goodbye." I propped my hands on my hips and glared. "*The library?*"

He twisted his fingers together, looking very worried, his gaze darting down a side hall. Eureka! I turned in that direction, head down and determined.

The butler let out a strangled sound and followed after me. "Don't, miss. Stop. *Please* stop."

I threw open the first door I came to. It swung open with so much force it hit the wall. I stormed into the room—which was clearly the library, with its walls of books and inviting fire—leaving the butler to deal with the rebounding door.

Henry startled from where he lounged on a sofa with his back to the door.

"I'm sorry, sir," the butler pleaded. "She slipped away from me—"

Henry stood, causing what was in his lap to fall to the floor. "Get out!"

The butler obeyed, backing out the door with his head bowed, but I didn't.

I thundered forward with my finger pointed at him. "How dare you send your lackey to bathe me as though I'm a stray mutt!"

"You didn't follow the rules. You reek of *him*. I have no

use for you." He pointed at the door. "Get out of my house. Now."

"You left me no choice. You called last minute. I'd already cancelled on him twice in the last couple of weeks because you changed the schedule. I couldn't cancel on him again."

"You *can* and you *will* if you want to continue under my patronage."

"I don't understand how you could possibly smell him on me. I bathed thoroughly—"

"Not thoroughly enough."

I took a couple of steps toward him. "Henry—"

"Do I need to have you forcibly removed?"

That was when I noticed the object at his feet. His prosthesis. His gaze followed mine. I made a move for it, but he beat me to it, snatching it up and holding it behind his back.

"May I see it?" I asked.

"No." His body language told me that was a very definitive *no.*

"Please? I want to understand—"

"The only thing you need to understand is the money I pay you."

His words wounded. I was under no illusion about our relationship. Except that I was. I felt close to him in a way I hadn't experienced since my Johnny. Even with his gruffness and his secretiveness, Henry was good to me. He paid for access to my body, but gave me untold pleasure he didn't have to. He cared for me. I know he did. The words were in the way he touched me, the looks he gave me, and the way he made me feel. Even now, with his anger simmering in the air around us, his eyes were wounded. I'd hurt him by showing up here after being with Jack.

"I'm sorry." He stiffened as I drew to within inches of him. "I'm so sorry I broke your rule."

I could see the pain behind his anger. He didn't speak, but then he didn't have to. His countenance spoke for him.

"I'll never do it again."

"See that you don't."

"I'd like to stay. With you. I've missed you."

Something hot and aching flashed in his eyes. "No."

"I'll take a bath for you. Right now. I'll go upstairs and scrub with your soap so I smell like you." I reached a tentative hand out to touch his face. "Or you could wash me."

"Can you wash away the memory of smelling another man on you?"

Oh, yes. I'd hurt him. More than I'd initially realized. "What would you like me to do?"

"End it. With all of them."

I hadn't mentioned my parting from Aaron because it would've broken Henry's rule about not speaking of my time with other men. So I told him now. He didn't seem appeased at all.

"How many are left then?"

"Just Jack...and you."

"End it with him."

I nodded. "I will."

"Tonight. Right now."

If he needed this to prove my love and allegiance to him, then I'd do it. Even if that meant hurting Jack. I strode straight for the telephone on the table next to the sofa and dialed Jack's number. Turning to face Henry, I listened as the phone rang and rang. Jack moved slowly, so I knew to wait and be patient. He'd answer eventually.

After the fifth ring, Jack picked up. "Hello?"

"Hello, Jack. It's me."

Henry watched and listened with eyes blazing fire.

Jack's voice dropped with intimacy. "Ruby. I was just thinking of you and our time together today."

Our time included some acrobatics to account for his limitations in achieving the anal sex he'd been so enamored with since I'd shown him my book. I couldn't help the rush of heat that swept through me at the memory. Henry noted it, his scowl deepening.

"We need to talk," I started.

"Sounds ominous."

"I'm sorry."

"Just spit it out, Ruby." There was anger in his tone and some hurt too. It seemed I couldn't keep from wounding both of the men I cared for.

"I won't be able to see you anymore."

Silence. Henry crossed his arms over his chest, his glare still firmly in place.

"I see," Jack said evenly. "Can I ask why?"

"I'm seeing someone else." I couldn't lie to Jack. It would be a betrayal of everything we were to each other.

"I know you *see* other men. I don't know how many and I don't care. That's never been a problem for me except when you didn't have time for me. But I'm guessing it's a problem for *him*."

"Yes, it is."

"Is it about money? Because I can come up with more—"

"No. It's not about the money." Henry's eyes narrowed farther so I turned away from him and lowered my voice. "It's more than that."

"It's more with him than it is with me. Is that what you mean?"

"Yes."

"You love him."

"Yes."

"But you don't love me."

"I do, but not—"

"Not like you love him." His chuckle was an ugly sound that grated deep down. "I bet if I had his millions you'd be having this conversation with him."

"Jack—"

"Don't start pitying me now, Ruby. I couldn't take that on top of everything else. Not from you. Never from you."

"I'm sorry."

"Is he there now, listening?"

I looked over my shoulder at Henry. "Yes."

"Put him on."

"I don't think that's a good—"

"*Put him on.*"

I turned and held the receiver out to Henry. "He wants to talk to you."

He snatched it from my hand and put it to his ear. "What?"

I couldn't hear what Jack said to him, but his expression changed from wary to shocked to angry in a matter of moments. He vibrated as he listened. All the while he kept his sharp gaze on me. My body reacted as though he touched me, my nipples pressing against the constraints of my dress and my sex throbbing between my legs. He noted my arousal and crooked his finger. Being the obedient thing I was I went to him and stood there waiting for what he would do next.

He covered the receiver and whispered. "Take off your dress."

I immediately began working the buttons until it fell at my feet. The cool air of the room hit me, making my nipples harden even more. He slipped his hand between my legs and lightly stroked me. Despite his anger, his touch was gentle and coaxing. I widened my legs for him, giving him greater access. I could deny him nothing. I was addicted to him.

Although I knew that Jack and Henry knew each other, neither one of them had ever spoken of the other and I'd never gotten the story of exactly *how* they knew one another other than some connection with Jack's father. It was Jack who'd given Henry my name so I could only imagine how he felt in learning that Henry wanted to steal me from him.

Their conversation took some kind of turn and Henry immediately removed his hand and gave his back to me, stepping away and speaking in rushed whispers into the receiver. I shivered at the loss of his touch and wrapped my arms around myself. He hunched his shoulders, curling his body around the telephone. What was being said?

Whatever it was, it made Henry gasp and stumble back a step.

"You wouldn't," he said, his voice full of something I'd never heard from him—fear, real fear.

I stayed where I was, hurting for both of my guys. Maybe I should end it with both of them and walk away from the whole business. That thought had me shaking my head. I couldn't do that. I couldn't leave Henry. I didn't want to leave Jack, but I'd do it. For no one else but Henry.

He turned back toward me and raked his gaze over me. I couldn't decipher the look in his eyes. It was dangerous and yearning and tragic all at the same time. What did it mean?

After a few more words that told me nothing of the conversation, Henry ended the call. He stared at me for several long moments. Painful moments. I could feel his agony like a force in the room. Then he slowly began to take his clothes off. He started by unbuttoning his pajama top and letting it drop to the floor. All the while his eyes stayed on me, gauging, reading, expecting. What, I didn't know.

He hesitated at the waistband of his pajama bottoms, then yanked on the string.

Schooling my expressing, I maintained eye contact. It was near impossible to hide my excitement. This was it. He was going to reveal what he could never show me before. I wanted to go to him and tell him it would be okay. Nothing he could reveal about himself would change how I felt about him.

He loosened the waistband and pushed the pants down to his ankles, then stood straight and stepped out of them. I met his gaze and tried to put everything I was feeling into it —my love, my hunger for him, my concern and understanding. Most of all my understanding.

I knew his secret. I'd always known.

Henry was a woman passing as a man.

The thick thatch of hair between his legs did not hold a deformed or missing appendage that necessitated the use of his prosthesis because there had never been a male member there in the first place.

I moved toward him, careful to go slowly and not scare him. He was just as beautiful to me as he'd been before. Maybe more so.

When I reached him, I stroked light hands over him, beginning with his beautifully sculpted face and continuing down over his torso to his hips and down the front of his thighs and back up again, until I cupped him between the legs.

He shook, watching me. Tears glistened in his eyes.

He was wet on my fingers.

This was why he'd asked me if I'd ever been with a

woman. But in my eyes he wasn't female. He was Henry. It was as simple as that.

Keeping my hand where it was, I reached up to pull him down to me. I kissed him with everything I had in me. And even though I didn't entirely know what I was doing, I stroked his slick folds. He trembled. Suddenly his arms banded around me and he kissed me like he'd die without me.

I pushed him back until he hit the edge of the sofa, then tumbled down on top of him, ending up between his parted legs. I pushed them apart and took him in. I'd never seen the female sex before other than my own. Not in person. Not this close. He made a move to stop me, but I pressed on his thighs, letting him know I would not be deterred.

"Don't you know," I told him in a shaky whisper as I continued to stare at his sex. "That you're beautiful to me. Just the way you are. I want... I don't know what I'm doing. You're going to have to help me. But I want to taste you." I ran a thumb through his slickness. "Here. The way you taste me." I glanced up at him to gauge his reaction to my bold declaration.

Tears ran from his eyes into his hair. "Do it," he raggedly whispered back. "Put your mouth on me." He didn't say it, but I knew what he wanted. He wanted me to put action behind my words. He wouldn't believe me unless I showed him.

Lowering my head, I breathed him in just the way he'd done to me the first time I'd met him in his office. His scent was intoxicating. I closed my eyes in ecstasy. My first lick was tentative and inexpert, but his gasp and gentle hand in my hair spurred me on. He tasted like...like Henry. Sinking deeper into him, I placed hot open-mouthed kisses every-where I could reach. And then I really got into it, flicking my tongue into him the way he'd done to me. I used my fingers on him the way he'd done me.

I got drunk off it. Off *him*. His taste, the pleading tone of his moans, and the way his legs widened and his head fell back. His fingers tensed in my hair seconds before he cried out in pleasure. I sat back and watched him go through it. Tears still leaked out of his eyes like they'd never stop.

He was beautiful. And he was mine. All mine.

LESSON 9

Henry's cheeks were flushed, his eyes bright on mine. His chest heaved and he shuddered in the aftermath of the pleasure I'd given him. My face was wet from it just the way his had been that first day in his office. I did nothing about it as I crawled up his body and put my open mouth on his. It was carnal. It was forbidden. It was incredibly arousing. I pressed my sex to his to help ease the throbbing. Grinding against him, I tried to get some relief, but only ended up increasing my arousal.

I wanted him. I wanted him in a way I'd never had him. Finally there was nothing between us. No secrets. No more hiding. No more barriers. Our bodies pressed together like this felt like nothing I'd ever experienced. I wanted to be inside him and all around him. I wanted to drown in him and never come up for air.

Breaking the kiss, I climbed off him. He reached for me immediately.

"Wait," I told him. "Close your eyes."

A crease appeared between his brows, but he obeyed anyway and settled back against the sofa. As quietly as possible, I retrieved his phallus and strapped it on. It took some finagling to get the leather straps on tight as I was larger in the hips than Henry. There was something on the inside of it; something textured that rubbed against me deliciously. Now I knew how Henry had achieved his pleasure as he gave me mine. It didn't make me feel like a man the way it did Henry. It made me feel closer to him, understand him better. He was complex to be sure. But weren't the most difficult puzzles the most satisfying to figure out?

I took a moment to enjoy the sight of him all long-limbed and laid out for me. He was naked in more ways than one. My heart pressed against my rib cage, trapping my breath. He was beautiful. Perfect. More so now than ever before. We'd reached some kind of threshold tonight and crossed over to the other side.

I wanted to ask him why. Why did he share himself with me now? What had Jack said to him to get him to drop all of his defenses and show me who he really was?

Did I really want the answer to those questions or did I just want to accept that he'd finally come around? Because I knew. I'd always known his secret. I'd known and hadn't cared. He was more to me than his parts, or lack thereof, more to me than the money he paid me, more to me than the pleasure he gave me. He was, quite simply, *Henry*. Perfect in his imperfections, his quick temper, and gentle hands. Perfect in his total domination of my body, my mind, my *soul*.

I lay down on top of him, careful to tuck the phallus off to the side so he didn't discover it yet. The feel of him, his bare flesh against mine. I hadn't realized until this moment how much I'd missed it and craved it even though I'd never experienced it. I took a moment to just lie with him and nuzzle that spot just under his jawline.

"I smell like you now," I told him. "Every time I take a breath, I breathe you in."

His arms came around me, his hand slipping into my hair the way I liked. "Now you know why I spent so much time between your legs. Can I open my eyes now?"

"No." I slid a hand into the curls between his legs. "I'm not done with you yet. You've been hiding from me and I intend to punish you for that."

"I wasn't sure you'd accept me..."

"Accept you? Naughty boy, I worship you."

"You still see me as a man?"

"Isn't that what you are?"

He wrapped his fingers around my wrist and worked my hand against his slick folds. "Am I?"

Gripping his wrist, I stopped his motion and drew his hand up above his head. His eyes remained closed. I had a feeling it wasn't obedience. He was still hiding from me.

"Of course you're a man, Henry. What else would you be?" With that, I reared my hips back and plunged into him.

His eyes popped open in shock. He wasn't hiding from me now. He stared wide-eyed up at me as I stroked into him.

"You're *my* man," I told him. "Nothing's changed. Don't you see that? You're my Henry and I love you."

"Oh, god, Ruby." His arms banded around me hard. He accepted my inexperienced thrusts, tilting his pelvis as though he couldn't get enough. "Make me yours. *Please*."

I lunged at him over and over, coming closer and closer to the brink of my own pleasure and trying to hold it off. I wanted him to go over first. His back arched and he cried out. I lost control then and ground against him, chasing my own release. We came together perfectly entwined and pressed together. Me and my Henry.

A long time passed before I caught my breath enough to ask. "What did Jack say to get you to share with me?"

He didn't answer for several minutes, playing with strands of my hair. Our sweaty skin cooled and our heartbeats settled in to a steady rhythm before he finally answered, "He threatened to tell you himself."

I knew he had, but I wanted to hear it for myself from Henry. "Would you have ever shown me?" I propped my chin on my hand on his chest to look into his eyes for the truth. "Or would we have gone on forever the way we had been? Did you think I was too simple to not figure it out?"

"I don't think you're simple."

"Yes, you do. Or you did. When I lie with men, they leave their seed inside me. You left me dry. I figured that out the first night we were together. Remember? Somehow you achieved pleasure from wearing your phallus. Did you not think that I'd figure out that you didn't wear it because of some injury or birth defect? That it served another purpose other than pleasuring me? Or these scars...?" I traced the half-moon shape a couple of inches beneath his right nipple. "Did you think I wouldn't catch on as to why you have them?"

"No. Yes. I don't know. I didn't think." He caught my hand and laced his fingers with mine. "I just wanted you. From the moment I saw your reflection in my office window. You were even more beautiful when I turned around. And so compliant. You took off your dress without hesitation and lay down and let me do things to you. Whatever I wanted. Your cries of pleasure were beautiful and your taste...like honey on my tongue.

"I still have the handkerchief I wiped my face with in my desk drawer. I take it out from time to time and touch myself to the scent and my memories of you and your body, the way you give yourself totally to me. No demands. Only pleasure. You take what I give you and don't ask for more. It's enough. I'm enough. The others... As soon as they got a hint that something wasn't right, their hand was out, asking for more money, threatening to expose me. Not you. Never you, Ruby.

"I had to take the chance even under threat that you'd stay true, and you did. You did." He crushed his mouth to mine with a desperation I'd never felt from him before.

I accepted the storm that was Henry, the things he said and the things he couldn't yet say. His kisses slowed and gentled. When I finally raised my head, well, I'll never forget the look on his face. He may not have the words yet, but I could feel them and see them.

I stroked the hair back from his forehead. "My Henry. My big, sweet man. I have all I'll ever want or need right here in this room."

"*Your* Henry. I like the sound of that. You don't know how jealous I was of your *Johnny*, the way you spoke about him. I wanted that wistful longing in your voice to be for me and only me."

"I'll always love him. I can't help it. And I can't help the way I talk about him."

"What about Jack? Is he *yours* too?"

"You heard me tell him he wasn't. You made me hurt him, so he hurt you. Or tried to. That really wasn't fair of you. I'm cross with you about that."

"You still want him?" Jealousy was there in his question and a fair bit of resentment. "He can give you something I can't you know."

"What could he give me that you can't?"

"Children."

I hadn't considered that. I'd always wanted a child. My

Johnny and I had been working on that very thing before he'd shipped off. Unfortunately we hadn't been blessed.

Never having children. I couldn't fathom it.

"We could adopt," I offered, a seed of worry planting itself in my belly. Was Henry looking for a reason to keep himself apart from me even now?

"You don't ever want to carry a child of your own, have it grow inside you, nurse from you, have your eyes or your nose?"

"Yes." I couldn't help but be honest with him. It was all I'd ever been with him. "I want that very much. But wanting it and having it are two different things. I wanted a child with my Johnny, but we weren't blessed. If we'd never been blessed, I'd have had this conversation with him. Do you want children?" I held my breath, waiting for his answer.

"Yes, but that's not likely to happen in the normal way. I want to marry you, Ruby. I want to live with you and lie with you at night, wake with you every day. I want to make you mine in every way, but I can't be that selfish. You deserve to have your dreams come true."

"My dream *has* come true. I never thought I'd find some-one, love someone after my Johnny."

"If my secret was ever discovered it would ruin you."

"I've been ruined. When my father cast me out. When my Johnny was killed. It didn't stop me from trying to be happy."

"This isn't the same. There are laws—"

I pulled away, slid the phallus out of him, and rose to my knees between his legs. "If you don't want me," I motioned between us, "or this, then say so. Say so right now, but don't lie there with me inside you, thinking up reasons to put me off because you're afraid. That's just chicken and that's not you."

He jackknifed, startling me, and gripped my face in his hands. "I want you, Ruby, more than anything or anyone in this world, but you're too romantic to see what's right between is also what's wrong. I want to be selfish and take you for my very own, but I can't do that to you. Society won't forget or forgive what I am. What *we* are. There's a name for it, Ruby, and it's ugly. We're an abomination.

"You'd be giving up your dream of having children to live with a freak, a Frankenstein monster, not a man. I'm not a real man." When I shook my head he pressed on. "I'm not. I never will be. As much as I feel that I am, I'm not. I can't ask you to give up everything for me."

"Then what is this? Why did you start it?" I pushed his hands aside. "Why did you make me fall in love with you if you're just going to tell me it's not real and I can't have it? Why are you being so *cruel*?"

"I'm sorry."

I climbed off the sofa, knocking his hand away when he tried to reach for me again. "No. Don't touch me." My hands trembled as I tried to work the buckle on the phallus. I felt stupid for wearing it, for falling for this man, for believing in him. I finally got free of it and threw it to the floor. "Don't call me." Sweeping down, I retrieved my dress. "Don't come over. I need the man who made me feel beautiful and special, not this coward who torments me and turns my words against me. When you're ready to be that man again, let me know. Until then I don't want to see you." With that, I stormed out of the library.

The thud of Henry getting to his feet behind me barely registered. He didn't follow me as I tore through the house, my dress flapping open, not caring as I made my way to the front door. The butler met me there.

His gaze flickered over me briefly before flying up and

sticking to the ceiling. "The car is waiting in the drive." His tone said everything—everything he thought about me.

Of course the car was waiting. Not only did the butler not like me, he didn't have any more faith in us than Henry did. I dashed away a tear and thanked him as I was taught. Turning away from him, I redid the buttons on my dress, then opened the door and went down the walk. I thought I heard Henry's voice as the car took off, but I didn't dare look back for fear I was wrong.

And for fear I was right. I couldn't go back to the way things were. I couldn't take his money. I couldn't lie under him and not feel the things I felt for him. I couldn't pretend that we didn't share something secret and special.

Most of all, I couldn't pretend we might someday have everything I ever dreamed of.

LESSON 10

Loud thumping on my front door woke me. The sun barely showed through the curtains, too bright to be night yet too weak to be full day. The pounding grew insistent, joined by the shout of a male voice. Jack.

The disappointment washed through me, cold then hot. What was he doing here? Hadn't he done enough? Hadn't he opened up then ruined everything? Wasn't it *his* fault I lay in my bed alone instead of tucked into Henry's warm embrace?

I strode to the door, not bothering with a robe, and yanked it open.

With raised fist to knock again, Jack tipped forward then caught himself on the doorjamb. He was unshaven, his hair looked as though he'd run his fingers through it a thousand times. Or he'd just come from the bed of another woman. The rush of jealousy surprised me. I'd given him up, choosing Henry over him. It was stupid to feel such emotions after everything that happened last night. My unreasonable emotions only added fuel to my anger.

"What do you want?" I demanded. "Haven't you done enough already? You have to wake me and half the neighborhood too?"

"I'm sorry." And he looked it too, from the crease of his brow to the turned down corners of his mouth to the sheepish look in his eye. "You don't know what agony it was to wait till morning to come see you."

"Nor do I care. Go away, Jack."

"No, please. Wait. I have to talk to you."

"I think you've done enough talking for the both of us."

"He told you."

"Of course he told me. He told me everything. And you knew all along. What was it, a joke to you? Were you and Henry both playing me for a fool? What did you think I'd do when I found out?"

"No, Ruby, I swear. None of that. It's just that he needed you like I did, like Aaron did. Please let me in. Let me explain everything."

The curtains across the street at the Morris house twitched. I'd be the talk of the neighborhood by noon, answering my door to a man in my nightdress. The damage was done and I could see that Jack wasn't about to be moved from my porch. I knew him and his stubborn streak well enough to know that he'd stay rooted until he got his way.

"Come in." I opened the door wider for him to pass through. "Say what you've got to say then go."

He hobbled into the living room and sank down on the sofa. "Got any coffee?"

"What I've got is half a mind to dump the pot over your head if I had any. Say your piece already."

"Henry called me."

I stared at him in stony silence, telling myself I didn't

care what Henry did or didn't do. Or Jack, for that matter. The lot of them could have each other and rot.

"He told me what happened," he continued.

"What you *wanted* to happen."

"He should've told you all along, Ruby. You know he should've. He was doubly selfish not telling you then trying to keep you all to himself."

"So you're going to tell me what you did, you did for me, is that it?"

"Yes."

I deepened my scowl. "So he's the only selfish one here, is that what you're telling me? You blackmailed him to what? Protect me? Help me?"

"Yes."

"Oh, no, Jack. That was all for you, not me. You can try to convince yourself of that but you'll never convince me."

"He wants you back."

"So you're his messenger now? I don't care any more about what he wants than he cares about what I want."

"Please, sit down. Please listen to what I have to say, then I'll go and you'll never see me again if that's your wish."

I took the chair opposite him and crossed my arms and legs and waited.

"Henry's always been the way he is," Jack began. "Since a child he never wanted the things a girl should want. He hated dresses and frilly things. He'd cut his hair short, then take the whipping that came with it gladly. As soon as he could, he moved out, changed his name, first and last, moved to Los Angeles, reinvented himself. He built his fortune from nothing. But none of it mattered. His father had a heart attack the first time he saw Henry's picture in the paper. His mother took her own life shortly after.

"He paid for their funerals, but didn't go. I'm pretty

much all the family he has left." At my surprise, he quirked a brow. "Don't tell me you didn't notice some kind of resemblance. We're first cousins on his father's side. We've always been close. I was the only one he kept in contact with after he moved out west. I stayed with him for a time after I came back." He motioned toward his broken body. "He helped me recover and didn't let me feel sorry for myself. He, along with you, helped me realize that I was more than what I was missing. He helped me get an apartment and find a job. He gave me money even when I refused.

"Noticing the changes in me after meeting you, he asked and I told him about you, about that first time, about how you saw me as a man even when I didn't. That's how you saw Aaron too, he told me that once. Did you know that? Said he'd never felt more like a man than when he was with you. I could see it in Henry's face that he wanted that too. It's a gift you have, Ruby, looking inside a person and seeing not only who they are, but who they wish they were. You saw me. Aaron too. And you saw Henry. You saw him even clearer than I ever could. Did you know that?"

I shook my head, not wanting to let his words get to me. But they were. Of course they were. Turning my face away, I swiped at my tears and pressed my lips together, trying to harden my heart against him and the things he said.

"I knew you were falling in love with him, I think even before you did. And the secret weighed heavier. When you called, I knew he'd put you up to it, but I also knew that it was what you wanted. You love him. But your love was based on lies. I told him that. I told him that he *owed* you the truth. That he didn't deserve you until he told you everything. I did that for both of you. As long as your love was based on an illusion it wasn't real love, and was that the kind of love he wanted? The kind his parents had for him? Or the kind of love he paid for?

"You see, I did it for him too. I had to know your love was real, that you loved him for who he was. He needed to know that too, even if he wouldn't admit it. He'd always wonder. Always. And it would eat at him, Ruby, until it ate him up. He comes off as gruff and strong, but he's not, not deep down. He's fought hard to be who he is and it's taken its toll. He needs you, Ruby. More than he's willing to admit."

I whipped my gaze around to meet his, the boiling brew of emotions pouring out despite how hard I tried to keep it back. "But does he *want* me? He threw every reason he could think of at me for why I shouldn't want him, why we shouldn't be together. I shouldn't have to convince him. He has to want me too. I deserve to be wanted. I deserve to be fought for the way I fought for him. Sending you to do his work isn't fighting for me, Jack."

"He didn't send me. After you left, he lost it. Charles called me to tell me Henry had had one of his *episodes*."

"Who's Charles?"

He looked at me in confusion. "Henry's butler."

"We were never introduced. Not even when he ordered *Charles* to bathe me because I reeked of you."

"He *what*?" He shook his head sadly. "That stupid son of a bitch."

"My thoughts exactly."

"That self-sabotaging bastard. Jesus, he's in deep with you. I didn't realize. *God*."

"*He's* the one you feel sorry for?"

"Yes. No. I know how it must have seemed to you, but it's his reflex when he's wounded. Strike back quickly and brutally."

"Ruthless is what I'd call it. I can't live with that, Jack. I deserve better. I gave you up for him, and all he's done is throw it back in my face after he demanded I do it."

"He tried to kill himself last night."

Icy fear splashed over me. "*What?* Is he okay?" I started to get up, but Jack waved me back down.

"He is for now. Charles got to him in time, bandaged his wrists, and gave him a sedative. He was groggy, but coherent enough when I got there. He's sorry, Ruby. So sorry. And desperate. He even offered something to me he never would've normally."

"What?"

"I'll let him tell you himself. When he's well enough, he'll come to you, Ruby, and when he does, please don't turn him away. Please listen to him. He needs you, and I think you need him and what he's going to offer."

"I don't understand. What could he have to offer other than an apology?"

"You'll see. I told him I'd stay with you. He didn't want you to be alone." Jack painstakingly rose to stand.

He wobbled a bit before he got his crutch under him. It really was a miracle how well he was doing after his terrible injuries. To think that Henry was partly responsible for Jack's recovery. Jack being the biggest contributor of course. He made his way to my chair and put a finger under my chin, tilting my face up to his.

"Come to bed with me, Ruby. Let me hold you while you get some rest. We can go to a diner later for some breakfast. What do you say?"

"I should be mad with you, but I'm not."

He raised his face to the ceiling. "Thank the good Lord for that."

Playfully swatting his hand away, I rose and he wrapped his arm around me. "I've missed you, you know."

"No, I didn't know, but I'm glad about it. Come to bed now. And no taking advantage of me in my weakened state."

"Ha! You, weak?"

"I am around you, my Ruby. Weak in the knees, weak in the head, and most of all, weak in the heart."

LESSON 11

Jack made good on his promise. We returned just after noon to find Henry waiting on my porch, his hat in his hand. He glanced up as we pulled into the drive. My heart took a hard knock at the sight of him. So tall and strong, and so beautiful he had me blinking back tears. He raised a hand and I got a glimpse of white bandage. The tears came welling up anyway.

"Don't let him see those," Jack warned. "He'll take them for pity."

I touched my fingers to my lashes as I climbed out of the car so Henry wouldn't see. Jack was right. Henry would see them for what they were—pity tears—and all of this would be over before he got one word out. Jack had been cagey at breakfast about just what sort of offer Henry might have for me, no matter which way I pressed him.

Henry's gaze stayed on mine as I walked toward him. When we reached him, Jack put his arm around my waist. Henry noticed it, but kept his features schooled, showing no reaction whatsoever to Jack's hand on me.

"Hello, Ruby," Henry began. "I was wondering if I could speak with you for a moment."

I inclined my head. "Come inside. I'll put some coffee on."

While I fussed in the kitchen, Jack stayed close to me, frequently touching me, and even got so bold as to kiss me on the cheek in front of Henry. He wasn't trying to bait Henry—that was really clear—and Henry only smiled mildly when I checked for his reaction. What was going on here?

When we were all seated around the table, Jack and I turned to Henry and waited for him to say what he'd come to say.

Henry took a sip of coffee—for fortitude, no doubt—then cleared his throat and began. "I owe you an apology for last night. I owe one to Jack too. I'm sorry," he said to his cousin. "For what I forced Ruby to do." He turned to me. "I apologize for saying the things I said and for trying to twist you up. I'm sorry I made you give up Jack. Something I could clearly see hurt you." He cleared his throat again and tentatively took my hand. I let him. "I love you, Ruby. More than anything or anyone.

"I know I don't have a right, but I'm begging your forgiveness. It's your choice if you want to stay with Jack. In fact, if you do, I won't stand in your way. You could have a child with him, Ruby, just the way you'd always dreamed of. I want to marry you, but only if I can offer you everything you've ever wanted."

Jack took my other hand. "If you want us both, you've got us. If you want only one of us, you only have to choose and the other will walk away. I love you, Ruby, and I too want you to have everything you've ever dreamed of. I'd like a child with you. And with Henry, if that's what you want."

Henry placed his other hand on top of Jack's and mine.

I shook my head. "I don't understand. How would that work?"

"If you want us both, you have us," Henry said. "We could be a family. An unconventional family to be sure, but then nothing about you or what's between us is conventional, is it?"

"What he's trying to say," Jack cut in, "is that you'll choose who to be with and when. We'll share you the way we have been. If that's what you want."

"In the same bed?"

Jack laughed. "I love my cousin, but not in *that* way."

"No more jealousy." Henry raised my hand to his lips and kissed it. "I promise. I want to give you everything, Ruby. If that means giving you Jack and his children, then I'll give you that and more. I realized something last night. I need you with me more than I need you all to myself. I've offered Jack a room in the house down the hall from mine. We could make it work, but as Jack said, it's up to you."

The tears came for real now and there was nothing I could do to stop them. "Are you sure?" When Henry nodded I turned to Jack. "And you're sure too?"

"It was my idea to introduce you to Henry. I could hardly start having an issue with it now. Not when it means I might get to keep you."

"I don't know what to say," I told them.

Henry kissed my hand. "Think about it."

"Are you sure? Are you *very* sure?" I asked him. This was such a sudden turnaround for him I could scarcely believe it.

"I will be," Henry said. "I can't say I'll get used to it overnight, but I'll try. For you. Anything for you." He kissed my hand again.

"Jack, would you mind giving Henry and me a few minutes?"

He glanced at his cousin before rising from his chair. "Some fresh air would do me good."

I waited until Jack was gone before I pulled my hand from Henry's. "I don't believe you're really fine with this...I don't know...*compromise*, are you?"

"I can be."

"All of that jealousy, where will it go? I'm going to smell like Jack and like you. I can't take baths all day. How will this work?"

"I'm not exactly sure about that." He stared into his coffee cup. "It wasn't his scent on you. It was knowing you'd been with him or with Aaron, and them being able to give you what I couldn't. Last night? I'd spoken with Jack earlier in the day. He told me he'd just returned from seeing you. That's how I knew you'd been with him."

"You dirty rat! I nearly scrubbed myself raw, trying to make myself perfect for you! And then you sent your butler in to bathe me..." I gave him my fury and shame. "How could you? How could you mortify me like that? Like I was some dirty mutt who'd rolled in the mud then tracked it into your house?"

"I'm sorry. That was my own insecurity making me act like a jackass toward you." Taking my hand once more, he dropped to the floor on one knee. "I swear if you'll let me, Ruby, I'll spend the rest of my days trying to make it up to you. Please."

With my other hand, I pulled down his sleeve. "What of these? What am I supposed to make of these? Will I live in fear that one wrong move will send you back to the place where *this* made more sense than working things out with me? Because I can't live like that, Henry. I shouldn't have to and neither should you. I love you, but I can't live with that kind of pressure. I need to know you're going to be okay. That no matter what happens, we're going to be okay."

"I didn't cut deep enough. I wasn't even trying. My head was just so full of losing you…"

"So it was what? A cry for help? A tantrum? What?"

"I don't know what it was. It was stupid of me to even play at it. I know that now. Jack spent a good hour lecturing me for it. He said the bandages would scare you and I can see that they do. It's not as bad as it looks, I promise."

"I lost the first man I ever loved. I couldn't bear it if I lost you too, especially if it was you who chose to leave me that way. I'd never get over it. Please promise me you'll talk to Jack or Charles or me if you ever start to feel that way again."

"I promise. I swear it. Please don't cry." He put his forehead to mine. "I can't bear the thought of bringing you pain. At the time I only thought of my own. It was all I could think of."

"I can't bear the thought of you harming yourself. Please promise me that whatever happens, you'll never do it again."

"I promise."

"I love you."

"Oh, Ruby. I love you too." He kissed me with an urgency that more than proved his words. When he lifted his head, he smiled and thumbed away the last of my tears. "I should've said that last night instead of all of the other things I said."

"Yes, you should've, you silly man. That's the first time you've ever said it to me."

"It won't be the last. If you'll have me, I'll say it a thousand times a day, every day."

"I expect you to live up to that promise."

"Oh, I will. Never fear."

"Will you tell Jack to come back in? I've made my decision."

"Anything for you."

He rose and came back in with Jack. The two of them resumed their seats and looked at me expectantly.

"Jack, you know how much I care for you." I took his hand in both of mine. "You've been so good to me. I truly believe that one day you're going to find a woman who loves you, and you're going to have a good life with her, filled with children and happiness. But that woman isn't me."

"Ruby," Henry gasped.

"I'm in love with Henry, and while your offer is tempting I know I'll have everything I'll ever want or need with him. Including children if the good Lord should choose to bless us."

Jack nodded. "I thought that's the way things might go. You don't look at me the way you look at him." He glanced at his cousin. "The lucky son of a bitch."

"Are you sure?" Henry's voice was a thin wisp of disbelief and happiness.

"I'm sure." I kissed Jack on the cheek and released his hand. "Thank you for everything you've ever done for me. You've given me more happiness than one woman deserves and you've been good to me. I'll love you and thank you for it the rest of my life."

"But not in the way you love Henry."

"No." I shook my head. "Not in that way."

"Well then." He stood. "I'll leave the two of you to it. Be good to her," he told his cousin. "You ever hurt her, you'll answer to me. Got it?"

"I got it," Henry answered, but he was staring at me when he said it. Tears stood in his eyes. "Are you—?"

"I swear, Henry, if you ask me one more time if I'm sure, I'm going to clock you."

He pressed his lips together and shook his head.

"That's more like it. Now take me to bed and show me just how much you love me."

"Gladly, my Ruby. Gladly."

ALSO BY BETTY PAPER

Crazy On You

Captive

Tinsel

Piano Lessons

BETTY WRITING AS BETH YARNALL

Dangerous Lines

Lost

Saved

Fake

Real

Urge

Rare

Betray

Recovered Innocence

Vindicate

Atone

Reclaim

The Misadventures of Maggie Mae

Wake Up, Maggie

You're Mine, Maggie

Find Me, Maggie

Azalea March Mysteries

Killing It In Vegas

Crafting Unputdownable Fiction series for writers

Going Deep Into Deep Point of View

Making Description Work Hard For You

Some Like It Hot: Writing Sex and Romance

ABOUT THE AUTHOR

Betty Paper is the super-secret pen name of a USA Today bestselling and Rita® nominated romance author. Betty writes naughty things you want to read. She makes her home in sunny Arizona with her husband, sons, and their rescue beasts.

For more information about Betty and her novels please visit her website- www.bettypaper.com

facebook.com/BettyPaperAuthor

amazon.com/author/bettypaper

bookbub.com/authors/betty-paper